GOAL LINE

Harrisburg Railers, book 6

RJ SCOTT

V.L. LOCEY

Love Lane Books

Copyright

Goal Line (Harrisburg Railers #6)

Copyright © 2018 RJ Scott, Copyright © 2018 V.L. Locey

Cover design by Meredith Russell, Edited by Sue Laybourn

Published by Love Lane Books Limited

ISBN - 9781785646232

All Rights Reserved

Dedication

To my family who accepts me and all my foibles and quirks. Even the plastic banana in my holster.
VL Locey

Always for my family.
RJ Scott

Goal
LINE

── HARRISBURG RAILERS 6 ──

RJ SCOTT &
V.L. LOCEY

Love Lane Books

ONE

Bryan

K *eep your eye on Ten, he's trouble.*

That was all the text said, and I re-read it a few times as if more words would suddenly appear.

I don't know why I looked for affection in any text that Aarni sent me because, in my kind-of-boyfriend's own words, he wasn't the demonstrative type. And he would always point out that someone could get hold of my phone. Then they would know that Aarni Lankinen, the villain of the Arizona Raptors, wasn't everything he made himself out to be, that he wasn't the playboy who fucked every woman within his reach. That he had a boyfriend on the side, and that it was me.

The phone rang, and I answered as soon as I saw his name. Aarni wasn't the most patient guy on earth, and he liked it when I was fast to respond.

"Did you get my text?" Aarni asked without preamble.

"I did."

"Don't let me down now."

I got the feeling, as he laughed, that he expected me to do that very thing. I still wasn't sure what would count as letting him down. But given the kind of person I was—clumsy, quiet and only really focused when I was dressed for hockey—I kind of expected to fuck up.

The Arizona Raptors had chosen me in the 2014 draft, not long after my eighteenth birthday. I was the second highest ranking goaltender drafted that year, something to be proud of, I guess. But I'd not managed to stay up at NHL level, spending the rest of the time in the Raptors' development team in Tucson. Until last year, when I'd actually been a starting goalie after both main goalies had been injured.

I hadn't been stellar, and Arizona put me on waivers, leaving me vulnerable to being picked up by who the hell ever. My confidence had been rocked. I was a solid goalie for the development team, but the minute I got up to the primary team, NHL level, I choked. Why the hell did the Railers even want someone who hadn't lived up to their early promise? I assumed I'd attend this training camp, and that would be it. They'd push me down to the Railers' development team, and there I would stay.

Which wasn't a bad thing, except they'd taken me from Arizona and from Aarni and it was the first time I'd been really on my own.

"Hello? Are you even listening to me?" Aarni snapped.

"Of course, I won't let you down," I lied.

I'm a good goalie, I stop pucks, I can be strong and focused and stay in my own head to track the plays in front of me.

Still, Aarni knew about me what I knew about myself; I'd choke at NHL level just as I had for the majority of my time with the Raptors.

I'm not ready. I should go back down to the minors.

"Also, don't get comfortable there. They're not going to keep you for long."

"I know."

"And don't forget what assholes the Railers are. Don't trust them, particularly wonder-boy Rowe. Arrogant fucker."

I didn't see Ten as arrogant at all, but then I was basing my assessment on TV interviews, including the one he'd given with Jared when they'd announced their relationship. I'd been proud of Ten and Jared for doing that, and part of me, the dark, hidden, ruined part, was green with envy that they were able to be open with the world.

I'd said that to Aarni, but he'd reacted badly and hadn't talked to me for three days. His disappointment was a knife in my gut, and I hated every second of it. That was not happening again. He was right. Ten was a Stanley Cup Champion, a superstar, and if there had been NHL players at the Olympics, then he would undoubtedly have been on Team USA. No team would ask him to leave just because he had a boyfriend. It didn't seem to be hurting the Railers, and they had a growing reputation as being LGBT-friendly.

"Jesus Christ, Bryan, are you even on this phone call?"

I pulled myself back from the edge. Aarni had said something about Ten being arrogant.

"I won't forget," I spoke with confidence so he'd realize I was listening.

"And remember I'm not there to watch your back." He sighed deeply. "I worry there's no one to look after you when you attract trouble. Especially from defenders like Max van Hellren. Asshole should have been thrown out of that game against us for what he did to me. Fucker lost us the chance at a championship. So fucking pleased he ended up collapsing. He deserved it."

My chest tightened. Max wasn't part of the Railers anymore. He'd retired after the cup win, but Aarni was right. There would be other guys there to step up in his place. Aarni had been furious, with a side order of mean, over what Max had done to him, checking him into the boards. But he'd finally calmed down, said he'd show Max what was what the next time the two teams met. He'd been so disappointed when Max had retired.

But Aarni was a good guy. He was the one who'd gotten involved when the bullying on the Raptors had gotten to be too much for me to handle. When the guys in the toxic locker room got on my case. I'd only played a few games at that level with the Raptors and had fucked every single one of them up. They'd hated it, but Aarni had been there for me.

He seemed to know the point when the rest of the team pushed it too far, always stepping in just before I was going to run from the room. He'd helped me so much, but he was back in Arizona, so far away.

"I'll be okay," I murmured, fear gripping me again about the kind of things I needed to face with this new team.

"I doubt that." He sighed. "But you weren't enough of all that for the Raptors to keep you, so you have no choice, and there's nothing we can do about it, can we?"

"No."

He must have heard the desperation in my voice. I hadn't wanted the Raptors to give up on me, but that was hockey. One day I had woken up in Arizona as the backup to the backup, fucking things up, and the next day, the team had put me on waivers, and I was suddenly in snowy Pennsylvania.

"Good boy," was all he said, but it was enough.

He hung up, but those two words gave me a shot of steel to my spine, and I settled my breathing before opening the car door. Security had let me right through to the player parking lot, and my Toyota sat right next to a sexy red Porsche. My salary had taken a hike, up to three million for the two-year contract I had here, so I probably needed a new car.

Even if the Railers saw through me and sent me packing, I'd still have enough money to buy a car.

"Hey," someone called from behind me, and I immediately assumed that I was standing somewhere I shouldn't have been. The man was in a guard's uniform, tall, built and smiling at me benignly.

"I'm sorry. They told me to park there."

"Of course. Bryan Delaney, right?" he asked and extended his hand for me to shake, which I did immediately after wiping the sweaty palm on my jeans.

"Yeah, Bryan," I said when I realized I hadn't answered his question.

"Welcome." He thumbed at himself. "Name's Pete. They said I needed to keep an eye out for the new guy."

He dropped my hand, and I forced a smile onto my face, even though my stomach was churning. "Thank you."

"This way." He chatted on about the weather, life, hockey and something about his sister who lived in Arizona. By the time he dropped me outside an office, I knew enough about Pete to write a book. Thing is, his chatter stilled my nerves, and I wasn't going into this room blind. I knew the name on the door, Alain Gagnon, former goalie for Vancouver, and one of the best goalie coaches in the business. I'd skyped with him once in his capacity as Goalie Coach for the Railers after they'd claimed me off waivers. He'd seen me coming to the Railers as a positive thing, a *great* thing. All I'd seen is my failure at NHL level hockey with the Raptors, and I remembered going back to Aarni and needing to be held.

Of course, Aarni had said he didn't need to hug me, but he'd reassured me that, however I played, he would always have my back. I'd needed the comfort. His words of advice stayed with me even now.

I just want you to realize what you are and what your place on the team will be. Ten acts friendly, but he won't care about you like I do. Stan? He's had some lucky saves, and as for that fucker Van Hell-ren? You saw what he did to me in our last matchup. I wish you weren't so naïve, Bryan. It's unlikely you'll get many starts, so don't be disappointed when you get sent down to the minors.

I won't be disappointed. I'd promised Aarni, and I'd made a vow to myself not to get too excited and involved.

Pete knocked on the door, then turned and left but not before winking at me, which meant I was flustered when I stepped into the office, even more so when I was faced with a vast Russian grinning at me and pumping my hand.

"Pleased to meet," Stanislav Lyamin boomed and clapped me on the shoulder. Stan was a big goalie, broad, strong, tall. I was as tall, yes, but I wasn't solid as he was. He was a hero of mine, someone I revered, and he was here shaking my hand as if I was worthy of his time.

I shook Alain's hand as well. Alain gestured for me to sit, with Stan taking the chair next to me. Stan couldn't seem to sit still, wriggling in his chair, and he appeared to want to say something.

Alain shook his head and pointedly stared at him. "Go ahead, Stan."

Stan immediately turned in his seat, and I did the same until we were face-to-face. I had to be wary of this man. He was such a force on the Railers, and even though his English wasn't the best, he could be just as hurtful as the Raptors' goalie.

"Jets, February fifteen, you save big." He made shapes in the air with his hands, and I realized he was asking me about a specific thing. Something he'd done maybe? I'd played at NHL level, a grand total of thirty-six times in four years, and I remembered each game I'd played for the Arizona Raptors with clarity. Huffing, Stan pulled out his phone, scrolled a bit and then thrust it at me, shaking it so I would take it. I held the phone carefully and checked the screen and saw I was looking at myself.

Wait, was he talking about my save against the Jets? He couldn't be. I *had* to be the only one who remembered that game.

I'd pulled off the best save of my entire career, an odd-man rush heading right for me, a screen that was impossible to see past, but I'd heard what I needed to hear, the skates on the ice, the crack of the puck on sticks, and I'd instinctively known where to move. Luck had played a big part in that save, but somehow Stan knew about it and wanted to talk to *me* about it.

"I remember," I said as he waited expectantly.

"Much big," he announced and then sat back in his chair, arms over his chest, a wide grin on his face. "Much big," he repeated. "Is good times. No?"

"Good times," I said because he seemed to need a reply.

Alain laughed with him. "Well, now that the fanboying is over, let's get to work. Bryan, I want you to get out with Stan at practice today, get you used to the new ice. Coach Madsen has a defenseman briefing, and you'll attend that first." He shuffled papers in front of him and cleared his throat. "We have some work to do."

Of course, they had work to do with me. The Raptors didn't think I deserved starts, so I guess I was lucky another team wanted to take a chance on me.

"Yes," I responded.

"You are what this team needs." Alain leaned forward, staring at me so intently that it was my turn to squirm in the chair. "I want to be honest with you…"

Here it comes.

"I wanted you a year ago but obviously couldn't get you. I was shocked you were put on waivers, and we need a solid backup for Stan here. I'm excited to see what you can do."

"You are?"

Wait. Did I say that out loud?

Alain didn't seem to hear the surprise in my voice though, or at least he didn't react.

"I want to get started today, so you're ready for our first back-to-back, and I want you in goal. You ready for the chance?"

No.

"I'm honored to be part of the Railers," I said instead.

Stan opened the door for me and followed me out, and we walked straight into a gaggle of hockey players, milling about outside the goalie coach's office. I recognized everyone, and it was Connor Hurleigh, the captain at least for this year, who stepped forward. Everyone assumed Ten would be captain one day, but right now it was Connor who led this team.

"Welcome to the Railers."

I shook his hand and forced a smile. "Glad to be here."

One by one the group welcomed me, and I kept my responses simple. No point in giving anyone a chance to see anything in me that could be exploited.

Keep yourself to yourself, Aarni had warned me.

Some of the players' expressions held confusion at my quiet responses, but they didn't say anything. Maybe they were used to Stan, who was all noise and brightness.

Well, they wouldn't be getting that with me.

"Do you talk to your pipes?" Adler Lockhart asked. He was one of the best chirpers in the entire league, always with a witty response or a throwaway line that cut a player to the quick. Somehow, he was never caught and punished for instigating. If there was a fight on the ice, then you knew damn well Adler had something to do with it. I had to be careful with him.

"No," I said, and shook his hand over Connor.

"Oh." He sounded disappointed, and then he brightened. "Must just be the weird Russians then." He ducked when Stan shoved at his head, and I stepped back and away. This could get ugly. It didn't get a chance to, though, as someone skidded around the corner and came to a halt next to Connor. I was face-to-face with Tennant Rowe, skating phenom, and the object of most of Aarni's derision. What could I say to the man who was the face of the team and one of the brightest players in a long time?

"Ten," he said, out of breath, thrusting out his hand.

I was tongue-tied. Ten was pretty. If that was a word you could use about a guy. All angles, with a broad smile and bright eyes. He shook my hand and waited for my response.

"Hey," I said. That was enough to be polite and not enough to put me on anyone's radar.

I was shuffled down the corridor, to a door bearing Jared Madsen's name, and that was it. With Stan close to me, my first day as a Railers team member at hockey camp was beginning.

I wasn't nervous at practice. Not really. All I had to do was be out here, on a team fresh from winning the Stanley *freaking* Cup, and slot in neatly as the backup goalie.

No pressure.

I could fuck it all up, *I probably will,* and they'd trade me away. Not today though.

. . .

THE PRACTICE WAS intense but also different to the few I'd attended with the Raptors. This team was focused, but there was also a lightness in the banter I overheard. I didn't join in, only took my time in net, my Raptors helmet at odds with its scarlet and gold against the blue of the Railers practice jersey I wore over my gear. Alain pulled me away to work on my blocker side, always the weaker, and tapped my helmet.

"See if we can get you something different. You wear an Itech?"

"Yeah, a stock mask."

"You going to get a new design now?"

My helmet was generic and in the wrong colors. There was nothing more detailed in design on there, apart from the color that marked it as mine. There were no names or pictures or inspirational themes. Just references to the Tucson area, the standard saguaro amid the desert. Enough to get away with, and not enough to mean anything to anyone.

I'd once considered putting Aarni's name on it some-where, but he'd laughed when I'd said that. *The quickest way for people to know about us, and hell, why would you even do it in the first place?*

"I guess so," I said. I'd probably use the dusky blue of the Railers and maybe some generic views of Harrisburg. That way, when I was sent to the minors, it would still fit in.

"I'll tell Stan." He skated over to Stan, who was effec-tively batting away pucks from a determined-looking Dieter Lehman. He said something to the big guy, and even as Stan was talking, he was still blocking those damn shots. I'd never be as good as that. A familiar melancholy consumed me, and I shook my head to clear it. I was my own worst enemy according to Aarni, and he was generally right.

I will be as good. I can *be as good.*

Showered and dressed in my jeans and hoodie again, sneakers tied and jacket on my arm, I waited for Stan as instructed. He was taking me to see the artist who did his helmet, which was a study in strength, from the girders of iron to the steam of a massive old train. There was a starkness of imagery, softened only by the image of a tiny, fluffy rabbit and the name *Noah* under it in cursive. There was also a mountain scene and ice, it could have been any mountains, but they must've meant something to Stan. Various Pokémon were scattered across his face protector, so tiny I could hardly make them out individually, but against each one was a name. I recognized the words *Ten* and *Adler*, so this must've been a team representation or something.

"Is ready?" Stan boomed at me from behind, and I turned from checking out the helmet and followed him out of the door, straight to a van. Not a Maserati or a Porsche, but a mom's van, with a kid's car seat and brightly colored toys scattered everywhere. He unlocked it, and I climbed in, but he was called back by a player, Erik Gunnerson, a smiling man with impossibly curly blond hair. They talked, heads close together, and then after laughing, in a smooth move Stan leaned Erik back for a deep kiss, and I watched.

I couldn't have turned my gaze from them if I'd tried. Right there in player parking, Stan was kissing Erik. In front of the whole damn team and me. When they parted, Erik reached up and cradled Stan's face, gazing at him with such love and devotion. Stan said something, leaning down to get close to Erik, and then they parted with a final kiss. I pretended I wasn't watching, but I couldn't help but notice his huge grin.

Does Stan ever stop smiling?

"We go," Stan said, backing out of the space.

Erik climbed into the low Porsche next to my car, with Ten taking the driver's seat. When a skater earned what Ten did and had to keep up appearances, a Porsche is what they drove.

Aarni's voice filled my thoughts. *"One day people will realize Ten isn't all that and that he's all for show."*

I tugged my jacket around me as Stan turned up his stereo and Elvis blasted from the speakers. He was singing along, loudly and ever so slightly off-key. I wish I could say his innate happiness was inspiring, but I just felt it was sensory overload. By the time we pulled up outside the artist's place, I had a headache, and everything inside me felt twisted, awkward and wrong. When I saw it was a tattoo parlor, my heart sunk. Whoever worked behind those frosted doors would be young and fashion conscious and confident, all artistic and shit, and there would be me, the slightly awkward Canadian kid who wasn't going to be on the Railers that long.

And there was Aarni's voice in my head again.

Grow some fucking balls.

TWO

Gatlin

"Are you positive about this?"

I had to ask because part of my job as a tattoo artist is to make sure that my customers are happy with their ink, not just now but forty years from now. Getting a lover's name placed anywhere on your body as a permanent fixture is dicey. When you're nineteen and want that name inked onto your cock? Yeah, someone needs to sit you down and give you the fatherly talk. I wasn't a father, but I was an uncle, which was kind of the same, only better.

"I mean, are you really positive about this, Tim?"

The young man nodded vigorously. "I love Dixie."

"Yeah, I can see that you do, bud, but I loved my old boyfriend, Rex, too. Until the day I came home last year to find him moving out. When I asked him why, he said his feelings for me were waning and that he'd come to care about me as one would for a dog."

Tim blinked at me, his soft brown eyes growing dull. "That's harsh."

"Yep." I folded my arms over my chest, waiting for Tim's extreme love of Dixie to spur him to say she would never leave him. As his brain struggled with the shot of reality old man Gatlin had just laid on him, ELO played around us, filling my small personal area as well as the rest of the shop. "Here's what we're going to do," I finally said as Tim sat there looking like a dumbstruck opossum. "I'm going to give you a week to contemplate this idea. If you come back in seven days and are still committed to getting Dixie's name permanently inked on your dick, I'll gladly take your cash and do the work. Deal?"

He was crushed. I hated to be the one to bring him down, but chances were, in a year, he and Dixie would be done. Probably, she would feel for him as one does for a dog. Ugh. Fucking Rex. Someday I'd get over that parting shot. Or not.

"Yeah, sure, okay. Dixie was really excited about it though…"

He rose from the adjustable ink chair, which strongly resembled something from a beauty parlor, and walked out, his shoulders slumped and his steps shuffling. I ran my hands over my face and pushed up off the small stool where I sat on while doing ink work.

"Another dream crushed," Jess said as she slipped into my area, her blue eyes glittering with trouble. I glanced at my niece, frowned and then smiled. She was so much like me it was scary. My older brother, Garrett, often said if he didn't know I was gay, he would have sworn I'd slept with his wife and Jessamyn was the result.

"He'll thank me when Dixie crushes more than his desire to see her name on his prick," I replied, reaching up over my head to stretch my back. Things popped and cracked.

"Not every relationship ends like yours did," she reminded me as she walked around my workstation straightening the pictures on the mustard yellow walls. Jess was a punk goddess from her bright pink hair to her black combat boots. Tats that I'd done dotted her bare arms. Mostly bright inkwork intermingled with skulls and bottles of poison. Garrett was not at all impressed with the artwork on her skin. Guess it rankled his investment banker way of thinking. Which I did as well, but he'd had years to get used to a gay tattoo artist as his only living sibling.

"True. Only *my* relationships end like that." I glanced at the old clock on the wall, artfully arranged among pictures of gay couples from the forties. There were color photographs of tattoos I'd done on customers and a few framed tour posters from famous rock groups of the seventies. Along with a montage of artwork that had been applied to various masks I'd designed for Stan Lyamin, as well as several other professional goalies, all the work coming to me via Stan's recommendations and referrals. "I'm taking a hiatus from romance until I hit forty."

"That's another thirteen months. Your prick will wither up and blow away." She sat at my desk and began rifling through the bills.

"Hardly." I sighed, grabbed my personal stuff away from her, and let her open the store mail. She was a whiz at bookkeeping and organization. Which was why I'd hired her as soon as she'd turned eighteen and Garrett couldn't get over her working here instead of in the bank. "There's nothing wrong with living the quiet life of a monk."

"Monks don't jerk off daily."

"I don't either. I should fire you for that kind of insubordination." I leaned my ass on the folding massage table by the bookcase. Jess waved me off with the phone bill, then put her feet up on my desk, her short green skirt showing all kind of leg and the newest tat she'd had done two months ago, a large butterfly with a skull head and rainbow antenna. Garrett had been quite impressed with that one. If blowing a valve is considered being impressed.

"Hey, are we going to Skipper Joe's tonight?"

Jess and I both looked at the doorway. Woody, my part-time artist, slid into the room. He was a funny kid, same age as Jess at twenty-two, tall and skinny with bright red hair and a sharp nose, which was why I called him Woody instead of his given name which was Paul. I thought it was funny. Shame I'd had to explain the nickname when I'd first given it to him. Some days I felt so old.

"How did you get Skipper Joe's from 'insubordination'?" Jess asked, then handed the phone bill to me. I began searching for my reading glasses.

"Oh, you said 'insubordination.' I thought you said in some sub or other station which sounded kinky as hell." Woody was a recently out gay, streaking his way through the wonderful world of daddies, bears, and leather with a gusto that I sometimes envied. Oh, to be that vigorous after working ten hours. All I wanted was a beer, the Railers game on the radio, and a foot massage after work. God, that was sad. Maybe Jess was onto something, but clubs and random hookups were not for me. Not anymore.

"You need to do something about yourself," I commented as I patted down my old Levi's as well as my Aerosmith t-shirt. "Where the fuck are my glasses?"

"On top of your head." Jess snorted, then shot to her feet when the buzzer signaling the arrival of a customer went off. "So yeah, we could do Skipper Joe's. I'm feeling a little randy tonight."

"You two go ahead. I have no interest in spending time

in a gay club with sweaty twinks who think Ronnie James Dio is the second baseman for the Yankees."

Jess giggled and slid around Woody, who stood there looking all kinds of stupid. I sighed, pulled my glasses off my head, and stared right at my employee.

"Ronnie James Dio was a member of Black Sabbath, Elf, Rainbow, Dio." Woody made a face and shook his head. "Leave my space and do not come back until you can tell me the name of one Dio album."

I shook the phone bill at him, then slid my glasses on. Woody slunk out like a whipped dog. I peeked at the total for the shop's phone usage, grimaced, and then glanced up in time to see my work area fill with Russian goalie.

"Hello, Mr. Gatlin gunman," Stan boomed, throwing his arms wide, then gathering me to his chest for a bear hug that nearly flattened my glasses into my nose. "I am still making fun joke about name."

Stan pounded my back. I coughed out a weak reply, then wiggled free. I wasn't a small man by any means. I'm close to six foot tall, so no one ever called me Shorty, but in comparison with Stan, I felt like a resident of the Shire.

"Still a funny joke," I told the towering man with his arm resting on my shoulder.

"I know. I make many funny jokes. This is good one I make today for Tennant. How do make tissue dance?" I started to reply, but Stan ran me over. "Puts boogie into it!"

I snickered. "That's a good one." My gaze caught a flash of blue material lingering in the doorway. There stood a young man in a Railers hoodie, with brown eyes and a mouth that poets would write sonnets about. Tall and wide-shouldered, his gaze touching on mine before dancing away. Christ, the kid was stunning, his long arms and legs adding to the gangly, awkward aura surrounding him. Dark hair cut short accented a strong jaw. Those eyes though…

They were full of sad secrets.

"I have more jokes! Why is so windy inside sports arena? All many fans!" Stan howled at the truly terrible kids' joke. I smiled, then wiggled away from the exuberant Russian. "Adler buy me book full of funny jokes."

"Did you bring a friend?" I asked, taking my glasses off, so the kid didn't think I was so old I needed them to read the phone bill. The fact that I did was really neither here nor there.

"Yes! Is new friend and good goalie backup for Railers, Bryan Delaney," Stan informed me, taking his arm from around my shoulders so I could step to Bryan and shake his hand.

"Right, we picked you up on waivers from the Raptors. Good move for the Railers," I said as I extended my hand to him. He glanced at me, my hand, the wall, Stan, and then finally slid his palm over mine. His skin was damp with nerves.

"You follow hockey?" Bryan enquired, his voice soft yet deeply masculine. Quite appealing, to be honest.

"Not much else to do here in Harrisburg during the winter." I pumped his hand a few times, curious about how a hockey player could be so timid. Didn't they need to be outgoing and assertive to play such a violent and aggressive sport? This man was all kinds of contradictions in one sexy-as-hell wrapper. Not that I was interested in wrappers, of course. I pulled free from Bryan's grip and put a foot or two between us. "You two here for ink or just to visit?"

"We no make ink now. Maybe later when we train Bryan for Pokémon balls. Now we look for good artwork for making spifftastic mask like mine."

"Ah, okay," I made my way to my desk, flipped the

phone bill onto my laptop, shoved my glasses into the front pocket of my jeans, then turned to face Bryan, who was still in the doorway wearing a wild expression. "I'd be happy to work with Bryan on some sketches. I'll just need some basic information about what you want the artwork to reflect, any special logos or names, things like that."

Bryan shot Stan a wary look, then pressed his lips into a fine line which made me think he didn't wish to talk about this right now.

"If you'd rather, we can set something up for another time so you can have a think about it. Why don't you go talk to Jess at the desk, and we'll schedule an hour or so just to work out what you want?"

"Sure, yeah, okay." With that, Bryan spun and disappeared.

I glanced from the empty doorway to Stan. "He's a little shy, isn't he?"

"Oh yes, is much shy but is normal for new player. I too am shy and meek when I come to Railers."

"I find it hard to imagine you ever being shy." I sniggered as the phone rang out at the desk, the loud bell rolling through the shop.

"Pah, I am so much shy. Hide face in locker, only take out when stink of socks and skates turn skin purple and faint from holding breath."

Now *that* I could see. I chuckled at the man I'd come to think of as more than just a client. It was hard to not take Stan Lyamin into your heart once you got to know him. Pity the same probably could never be said about Bryan Delaney, he of the beautiful melancholy eyes. Not that I was interested in pretty, woeful eyes.

"So, tell me about the preseason," I said as we waited for Bryan to return. "How's it looking for that second cup run?"

"Oh, is looking much good." Stan flopped into the chair, his long legs splayed in front of him. "We make good moves during summer, like Bryan, and many of us work with Trent too for making faster skate moves. We are much graceful now."

"Yes, I bet you are." My gaze left Stan when Bryan reappeared. "Did we find a time that will work for you?"

"I uhm…tomorrow at eight?" He clutched a black-and-mustard yellow appointment card.

"That works. I usually break around eight for dinner. We can go across the street to the bar, have a burger and a beer, and talk mask designs." Giving him my most reassuring smile didn't seem to ease the tightness around his mouth, but Bryan did nod in reply. I glanced from one goalie to another. "Stan, you're more than welcome to join us."

"Oh no, I am not going out tomorrow. I am home body for my family. Is big night! New episode of *Doctor Marcus Welby M.D.*, show Mama loves."

I didn't quite have the heart to tell him that his beloved mama's show wasn't new at all. It was probably older than me.

"Okay, well, it'll just be Bryan and me then." My attention swung from the Russian flipping through sketches for tattoo ideas, to the young man who still had not stepped fully into my little workspace. Was he scared of needles? Not that I had any lying around. My shop was spotless; I made sure of that. All the Pennsylvania rules and regulations were followed to the letter.

"Right. Just us." Bryan edged out of the room when Stan stood up.

"Is all good news then." Stan offered me his big hand, which I pumped a few times. I gave Bryan a small nod and got a long look from under thick lashes before he returned the nod, then stepped out of sight. "You make helmet shiny new like four polished carrots for my new goalie teammate?"

Polished carrot? "Do you mean make it shiny like twenty-four carats?"

"Yes! Shiny like golden carrots."

"I'll do my best." I grinned, then lifted a hand in a wave. I stood there for a long moment, contemplating the newest Railer and the untold stories hidden behind those beautiful lashes.

"Hey, your next appointment is here."

I started a bit when Jess stuck her head around the doorway. "Right. Remind me what this one is."

"The girl who wants swallows bursting from a dandelion on her wrist."

"Great. More swallows."

"Did someone say something about swallowing?" Woody shouted from his little room next to mine.

"Is it time to go home yet?" I asked my niece. It had to be close.

"Nope. You have four more hours with us, lucky man!" Jess beamed, then went out to usher my next customer in. She was enjoying this far too much.

Shame I couldn't have cut out tonight to have a beer and a burger with Bryan Delaney. Generally, young guys weren't all that appealing to me, but there was something about him that made me want to get to know him better, touch him, ease the stress lines around his young eyes and stroke a finger over his bottom lip as he—

"I'm so nervous! Oh my God!" My client's chatter stopped me thinking. "This is my first tattoo. Will it hurt? This is going to be so cool! I love this idea! I saw it on Pinterest and said to Gail. She wants to watch and decide if she wants one that matches. I told Gail that was so my spirit, right? I mean, I always feel this feeling when I see birds fly by. Oh, wow, you have a lot of tattoos. What do they mean? They're so cool! My brother has barbed wire on his biceps, which I told him was totally out of style now. Do you think the dandelion blows could be watercolor?"

My God, it *had* to be midnight.

THREE

Bryan

_____

W e focused on movement drills for an hour, Stan working as hard as I was at finding his focus. He talked a lot as we practiced the movements over and over. Not to me at all, but to the ice and the pucks.

At one point, I swear he called one of the pucks Doug, but I wasn't going to ask if I heard things, right? Because goalies were odd.

I guess I was odd as well, although what classified me as different wasn't quite as apparent as Stan. I didn't talk to my pipes, or pucks, or make chicken noises every time a player shot at the goal and I stopped it. I didn't keep my eyes closed when I was in a game or anything, but I didn't only rely on vision, and that was the crazy in me. I listened, over and above the noise of chirping, and music, and the smack of pucks into the glass behind the net. I could hear the weirdest things.

No one had ever said this to me, so I guess I was unique, but ice sounded different depending on a hundred different factors. Every time I stood in net, I stooped to touch the ice, just the tip of my gloved finger, and to anyone watching it would appear like a simple stretch, but it was way more than that.

It was a connection, an understanding between us that the cold surface would feed information to me the whole time I stood there. The crack of a puck was ignored when the whispery scratch of skate on ice made me relax. This was Ten, heading my way. I didn't even have to check around Arvid 'Arvy' Ulfsson, the six-foot-five Swedish defenseman who was blocking my view, as we worked on game vision. The idea was that Arvy would be an effective screen, and I wouldn't see Ten enough to get a hold of angle.

But I heard Ten. I didn't know how it worked, I couldn't explain it, but I *heard* him.

He was a brilliant skater and has this quiet way of using the space around him, not all flashy and showy but determined and focused. I'd watched a lot of tapes of Ten over the past few weeks, since finding out I'd be with the Railers.

The thing about Ten was that he wasn't predictable. He wasn't the guy who always shot from the left. He was the one who danced and dangled and then did a one-eighty and went backhand. I'd seen him knock a puck from the air, hold off two defensemen, using his foot to corral a bouncing puck and then shoot glove side on a confident goalie and still find that small gap to get the puck into the net.

He was variable, so there was no surefire way to counter his shots.

I had to have patience and wait until the last minute. Listen for the whisper of his skates and take into account the way Arvy moved so I could make an educated guess on Ten's position.

Arvy was good, though. He didn't move a muscle.

For me, it was all about reaction, not only drop and stop. If I fell to my knees, blocker to the floor, stick protecting my five-hole, then I was sure to let in a goal that would clear my head.

I had to out wait Ten.

When he made his move, I was there, stopping the puck in my glove and curving it, so I slammed it to the ice, no chance of a rebound goal. I let out a *whoop* of glee.

They may have been conditioning shots, but I had stopped a goal from Tennant *Freaking* Rowe.

Shit. I stopped Ten.

Everything stilled in the arena, or was it me? Was everyone looking my way? Warning me not to mess with their star? I glanced past Arvy at that instant to see Ten circling back.

Fuck.

He grinned, stick-tapped my pad, the age-old sign of recognition, and laughed. "Nice," he said and skated back to the rest of the team.

Arvy turned as well and winked. "Keep it up."

No one was pissed I'd stopped Ten, or at least they wouldn't show it on the ice, and for a moment I allowed the elation to fill me before I settled back for the next shot, this time from the captain himself.

Few positions on the ice can compare to the goalie. Goaltenders can be hailed as heroes or scapegoats, depending on the outcome of each game. At that moment, I felt like a hero.

How stupid is that?

Connor got a shot past me, as did a couple of the others, including Ten's second shot, and his third, and fourth, but I was doing good, and Stan did nothing but grin all through practice as we swapped in and out of the goal.

I was waiting for the other shoe to drop, but I was sure as hell going to enjoy feeling competent while it lasted.

I NEEDED TO FIND AN APARTMENT. The Railers had put me up in a hotel until I found something, but even as I sat and made a list of what I wanted for the team realtor, I was reluctant to ask for anything fancy. I just needed a bedroom, a small kitchen, and a large living room that I could do my stretches in.

And a TV. That would be good. I hadn't gotten my music system out of storage since I'd left my billet home. It was still there. My Yamaha amplifier, CD player, Mission speakers, and Rega turntable had been lovingly boxed up and put away, even though my billet parents had said the system could stay in my old room. They hadn't understood why I'd wanted them to have an empty place they could use for another junior hockey player who'd need them as much as I had.

I'd made Daisy Jacobs cry when I'd said that.

Daisy and George Jacobs of Erie, Pennsylvania, *are* my real parents. Not by blood. Emma and Tom, their children, aren't my siblings in real terms. But they are the only people I will ever call family, and they'd saved me.

And yeah, it sounds dramatic when I say they'd saved me, but they had. They'd offered me a home that was filled with love and laughter instead of the strict religious control of my own family and the alcoholic father who liked to use me as his punching bag. Hockey had been my way out of that life, and through that, I'd landed in the best place possible. I needed to hear Daisy's voice.

I thumbed through my contacts and connected to Daisy, who answered on the first ring. I imagined her standing in her office, with its views of the Jacobs' yard, their huge Newfoundland, Beck, asleep in a loose sprawl at her feet. I could picture it so easily that it hurt.

"Tell me everything," she demanded by way of introduction. "Is Ten as sexy in real life as he is on TV?"

"I'm not telling you that," I teased back, and I could imagine her pouting. She had a healthy love for Swedish goalies who played in New York, and, it seemed, Tennant Rowe.

"How are you, sweetheart? How did your first days go? Tom said he texted you last night, but he wasn't sure if you got it."

Guilt poked at me. Daisy had this way of saying "you should have texted your kind-of-brother back" without actually saying it.

"I didn't see it, sorry. They're running us ragged." I wasn't entirely lying. I *had* seen Tom's text, but the Railers were intense about this conditioning work, and I was exhausted. Still, I'd also seen the two texts from Aarni and replied to those pretty quickly.

Boyfriends are different.

"I have to learn the process," I added.

"He understands. I just wanted to let you know we're all so happy to hear from you."

She instinctively knew I needed that reassurance because that was the kind of mom she was. At the age of fifteen, I'd been playing in the Ontario Hockey League, and it was hundreds of miles from my real parents. I'd needed an American billet family in Erie, Pennsylvania, someone to live with, someone to look out for me. I'd lucked out with George and Daisy, who, after a while, I trusted enough to tell them all about my birth mother and deadbeat father. Yep, they knew all about my previous family life. If you could use the word family. Or indeed, life.

"I need to find an apartment in Harrisburg." I deliberately changed the direction of the conversation before she began talking about how she missed me. It had been a few years since I'd left their home. I saw them as much as I could, but I couldn't bear to discuss how much they all loved me, or in turn, how much I missed them. Not today.

"Don't the Railers have someone to help?" Daisy asked.

"They do, but I'll need to give them a list of what I want."

"Somewhere to sleep, eat, and stretch, am I right?"

This was an easy conversation, and I resolved to text Tom back as soon as I got off the phone with Daisy.

"Mostly that," I agreed, and then I went quiet.

"Sweetheart, is everything okay?"

I could've lied. I could've said that everything was fine, but it wasn't. How was I going to cope without having Aarni close by? Who would run interference for me with everyone else? How was I going to deal when the day came for the Railers to realize I was an easy target?

"No," I said. I couldn't lie about the things that mattered, not when it had been Daisy who had taken me to every single one of my appointments with the counselor when I'd first arrived in Erie. She'd held my hand when I'd let her, and hugged me if I was desperate, and she never called me on any of it. Daisy Jacobs was there for me the entire journey to the NHL draft and then to that single awful point when I had to leave them behind and become an adult.

Thank God I found Aarni to look out for me.

"Do you want to talk about it?" she asked in her softest voice.

I didn't very often want to talk about things. What was I going to say? This wasn't the first day at a new school;

this was a professional contract with a Stanley Cup winning team. This was real goddamn life, and I wasn't some kid who needed the closest thing I had to a mom to cuddle me and talk me off the ledge.

"I don't know," was about the best I could come up with.

"Oh, honey, did you get another letter?"

Just thinking about the essays I'd received from my birth mother, warning me about hell, and God and fuck knows what else she thought up, made my chest hurt. She wouldn't let it go.

Can't let me go.

As far as she was concerned, I was going to burn in hell for my deviancy, and she had to save my soul. They arrived regularly as clockwork, chatty missives about how well my birth dad was doing at work, how the priest asked after me and worried about my soul burning in hell. How Darren had gone to conversion therapy and had now settled with Gina, the daughter of the local car dealership owner.

I closed my eyes as pain washed over me, and thoughts of Darren and what he'd gone through were front and center. He'd called me once, a long time after I'd left that first home, with the cruelty of my mother's church a burden I couldn't bear. He'd left a message on my phone, told me not to phone, told me goodbye, added that he'd found a way to be 'normal' and hoped I did too.

I tried to call him, but he never answered, and a couple of days later, the number had been disconnected.

"Bryan? Did you get another letter?" Daisy asked again, this time with rushed concern in her tone. She knew what I'd been like when they first started to arrive, had seen how they destroyed me each and every time.

"No. No letter." I thought on my feet. "I'm just nervous at a new team."

She let out a small sigh of relief. "Just remember, they're as nervous of you as you are of them."

She always said that about every drama in my life. It made me feel better, reminded me of moments with hot chocolate, warm store-bought cookies, and her gentle voice.

Aarni wasn't impressed with me having that connection to the Jacobs family. He called it odd how close I was to people who weren't even related to me. He'd never given me a convincing argument as to why I should stop thinking about them or treating them like my parents. So, I kept them to myself. It was the easiest way.

I certainly never told anyone that they'd saved me.

I told people I loved the Jacobs family as much as my own, but I was lying. I loved them more, completely, and the day I'd left their house, I cried. I'm supposed to be this strong hockey goalie, but when I was drafted by the Arizona Raptors, I sobbed in Daisy's arms and demanded they all move to Arizona with me.

They didn't, of course, but they were always only a call away, and when I was working hard in the Raptors' development team, they came to as many games as they could. I played *Fortnite* with Tom every chance I got, even when I was with my first professional team on tryouts in Arizona and he was at college in Seattle learning to be something very important in criminal justice. Emma used to text me at least five times a day, trying to set me up with her friends, all of whom were "super cute" and "loved" hockey. She had a boyfriend now, and I knew what that was like, so I understood why she didn't talk to me as much. I missed her texts though.

I glanced at the clock, knowing I had to go to my meeting with the tattoo artist, pushing down the worry and focusing on what Daisy was telling me, about Tom, Emma, George, and Beck.

"We're so pleased you're back in Pennsylvania," she said. "We're only four hours from you, so expect lots of visits. Will we see you before the season starts?"

"Soon," I said, and then after an emotional exchange of *love you* and *miss you*, and a promise of sending me a gift, I finished the call with about thirty minutes left until my meeting.

Daisy wasn't precisely the baking kind of mom, but she sent me other things on a frequent basis, like gift cards for food, and letters that told me every piece of news she could think of. Last month, she'd sent me a tin of store-bought cookies she'd put in a tin that had belonged to *her* mom. I hadn't opened the tin, because the air trapped in there was from the only home I'd known, and I didn't want to let it escape.

That was how bad I had it. Some days I was consumed with the despair of my *family* being too far away.

I'd showered at the practice arena, so I pulled on clean jeans, a mostly fresh shirt, and one of the many Railers hoodies I'd been given. I'd agreed to be number thirty-one, the numbers large on my back, and a weird part of me didn't miss the number thirty I'd had while playing in Arizona. This was a fresh start.

Aarni texted me a photo of his dinner, steak and fries, and a half-finished bottle of wine. It was followed by a selfie, of him with his arms around a blonde woman who had a wine glass in her hand and scarlet lipstick on her lips.

I hated her. I hated him for sending it to me.

No. I don't. I love him.

Even if he doesn't love me quite the same.

. . .

I'D FORGOTTEN where we were supposed to be meeting, and that put me on edge. Was I supposed to go straight into the tattoo place itself or meet the artist in the bar? I knew his name, it was on the card, and it wasn't a name I'd heard before—Gatlin. That I did know, but I was on edge. There was something about the man from yesterday that unnerved me. Possibly, it was his tattoos. I'd seen sharks, turtles and other Polynesian ink that extended past his wrist onto his left hand. The ink work on his right arm was more colorful. Staring had seemed rude, so I'd only gotten peeks here and there. It could have been the quietly confident way in which he stood and talked to Stan, his light blue eyes focusing on me every so often. Or the way he'd smiled at me and waited for me to speak to him. He'd asked me questions about names I wanted on the helmet, or images, and that had unsettled me as well. Or I could've been feeling nervous just because I'd forgotten where we were to meet and now stood on the sidewalk outside his shop looking like an idiot.

I decided the shop was the best bet, but before I could move, he opened the door from inside, a ready smile on his face and his hand extended.

"Hey, Bryan."

I took his hand and shook it, and then he juggled a sketchpad and pencil case and closed the door behind him.

"Hope you've brought your appetite. They make the best burgers here."

We walked to the bar, no more than thirty steps, and I must admit, from outside, it didn't look like the best place to eat, but as soon as I set a foot inside, I felt at home. Probably due to the fact they were playing Queen, and the waitress grinned at Gatlin as if seeing him made her day. He pulled her into a quick hug, and we followed her to a table in the corner, right next to an old jukebox. I didn't immediately sit, taking the time to glance at the playlist. From Queen to The Beatles, by way of Dire Straits and Black Sabbath, there were no bad songs that I could see.

For all the shit I'd grown up with until I was fifteen, I'd had access to a library of vinyl records and an old HMV record player. Music had been my escape.

The jukebox had apparently been set up with a playlist already purchased, as it slipped seamlessly from Queen to Black Sabbath, and I nodded along to the beat for a few seconds before slipping into the chair opposite Gatlin.

"You like Sabbath?" Gatlin asked, shock in his voice. I immediately felt defensive and pushed that down when I realized I was just about to freaking apologize. "How old are you?"

I lifted my chin. "Nearly twenty-three, but I have all the Sabbath albums on vinyl."

Gatlin sat forward in his chair, "Even their live recordings, like *Live Evil?*"

"Yep."

He moved back and exhaled with a whistle. "Nice. One day I'll have to come over and listen."

I swallowed. "My turntable and deck are back in Erie, and all my records."

Somehow, I'd shut the direction of that conversation down. I had to be careful; Aarni said I was too trusting, and I didn't know Gatlin at all.

"That's where you're from originally?" The conversation was interrupted by our waitress filling water glasses and pointing us to a board for menu choices, which seemed to be limited to four options. "My usual," Gatlin said and stared at me expectantly.

"Chicken," I said, and she left us alone again.

He opened his sketchpad, and in a few deft strokes, he had created a simple helmet shape. "So, something for the

Railers?" He was leaping ahead, detailing steam and iron, then took out a blue pencil to shade, and all I could do was stare at his bent head. He had short, light brown hair, the same brown in his beard which had liberal amounts of silver in it as well. It was difficult to tell how old he was, although the gray implied he was older than I was by more than a few years. His skin seemed soft, his forehead furrowed in concentration, and I knew when he looked up I would be staring into the kindest blue eyes. He was the complete opposite of Aarni. He was slimmer; he had more tattoos, obviously, and gray in his hair.

Aarni has kind eyes as well.

No, he doesn't. They are fire and passion, not kindness.

I shook my head to clear it from thoughts of comparing Gatlin to Aarni. I was with Aarni, and I was loyal to a fault, despite the image of the blonde woman draped over him tonight. He was the kind of man who needed other men and women to love him. I just needed one man. That was how our relationship worked.

"Family? Parents, siblings?"

I realized that Gatlin was staring at me again. "No." I was immediately on top of that one before I realized what it must have sounded like. "I mean I have them; I just don't want them on…" I waved away the rest of the sentence. His expression was puzzled but only for a brief moment, and then he smiled again.

"Hometown?"

I thought about the place I was born, in the middle of nowhere Canada, with the woman who I'd called Mom.

"No, I don't want that."

He nodded as if he agreed, then tapped the sketch-book. "The design is entirely up to you. This is your helmet, your design, your loves and hates, the things that are special to you. What makes you tick, what is the essence of you. I want to see inside you and get a real feel for who you are."

I blinked at him. That was way too deep, and I felt nauseous.

"No," I said.

And left.

FOUR

Gatlin

W hat the ever-loving *fuck?*

Our server arrived with our dinners. She stood there with two platters of food, looking a great deal as I did, I imagined.

I threw her a quick glance, smiled despite the surge of anger I felt and pushed to my feet.

"Tina, can you take those back to the kitchen and keep them warm?"

She nodded as I went off in pursuit of the hockey player with the bad manners. I found him heading west and jogged to catch up.

"Hey, pretty boy!" I shouted.

He never paused. He just hurried along, his head down as if he were expecting a piano to drop on him. I ran a bit faster and caught up with him in front of a mattress store that had recently closed its doors. "Hey!"

I grabbed his arm. He spun around, his eyes wide, his arm coming up defensively. My fingers slid from his sleeve.

Bryan blinked at me as if he was shocked to see me glowering at him.

"I have to go," he said, then checked past me to find the most direct path to somewhere, his car probably. I put myself between him and his escape route. Sure, he was taller by a few inches and had about fifty pounds on me. Also, he was much younger and an athlete, so he could've easily tossed me aside if he'd wanted to. But something deep inside told me that he wasn't prone to violence. He had experienced it though if that knee-jerk reaction to my touch on his arm was any indication.

"You can go after I have my say," I stated, folding my arms over my favorite Emerson, Lake & Palmer t-shirt. Thank goodness it was a warm fall night, as I'd left my jacket back at the bar. He closed in on himself, like a morning glory closing its petals at dusk. "That was about the most unprofessional thing I've ever seen. You do realize that I took an hour out of my work schedule to sit down and talk with you, right?"

"Yes. I'm sorry."

I stared at him, startled a bit at how automated his words sounded.

"Well, yeah, you should be. I could have been making money."

"I'll pay you for your wasted time." He reached back to find his wallet.

"No, that's not what I'm after here. You just can't walk out on a business meeting. It's amateurish and frankly below what I've come to think of as the standards of the Railers players and organization."

A car went by, an old Blink 182 song rolling down the street as it passed. Bryan shifted his weight from one foot to the other. I waited. He lifted his gaze from my boots to my face for a moment.

"I'm sorry to have acted in any way that makes the Railers look bad." His expression was sorrowful. I'd seen dogs being scolded that didn't look that pitiful. Shit, okay, so now I felt like a dick. "I really want to go now. Can I go?"

My mind was struggling to keep up with all the wild input Bryan was shoving into it.

"Sure, yeah, if you want to go, then go." What else could I say? Not as if I could drag the man back to Binky's Pub and force him to talk helmet design with me. "You know where to reach me if you decide to try this again."

He nodded, his gaze flying to the empty storefront behind me. I watched him hustle off, his shoulders up by his ears as if he were cold, but the night was far from chilly. It felt as if I stood there on the sidewalk in front of Bargain Barney's Bedding for a long time pondering what it was I'd been a part of. Somehow, my righteous indignation had sputtered out in the face of Bryan's... what was it exactly? Fear? Anxiety? Conditioned response?

I made my way back to the pub, thoughts churning over what had happened. Our waitress had thoughtfully put our meals into takeout containers, so I paid and tipped her and made my apologies before heading back to the shop. I had a nine o'clock appointment, but he wouldn't be there for another thirty minutes. I walked through the front door and into the shop, then stalked up to the counter and dropped the bag of food in front of Jess. She quirked a pierced brow.

"My dinner companion ran off," I told her while opening the big brown bag.

"Did you start talking about your obsession with Joe Perry again?"

"No, I did not." I huffed, pulled out the chicken dinner, and passed it to my niece. Judas Priest was playing, Rob's incredible voice soothing my jagged edges a bit. "I'm not obsessed with Joe Perry. I'm obsessed with Eddie Van Halen."

"Eddie *has* aged well." Jess sighed while taking the lid off a small cup of coleslaw.

"That he has. Anyway, no, I did not start talking about Eddie. I merely asked the kid what he wanted on his mask. We talked for a second about his family, and then he up and ran out."

I walked over to the far wall and flopped onto a couch. The purple walls were covered with tattoo designs on posters and papers that fluttered when I dropped down. Jess had overseen the new paint job last year. I'd have left the damn walls black as they'd been for years, but Jess had wanted some color in the shop. We'd gone back and forth for three months, and then I'd given up and let her have her way. Which was why I now owned a plum-colored tattoo parlor with areas painted anywhere from mustard yellow to some crappy orange tone to a pink bathroom. Pink. In a tattoo shop.

"Like he stuck you with the bill?" She cut into her chicken, the plastic knife making a pained squeak as it went into the Styrofoam.

"Well, yeah." I scooped up my burger and took a bite, my gaze flitting to the PS4 and TV in the corner. The game system gave folks something to do while they waited for their turn, which kept them happy.

"What a cheap cock," she mumbled around a mouthful of roasted chicken. "This is amazing chicken."

"It's not the bill issue that got me mad. Shit, I was going to pay anyway, because he's a potential new customer, and the fee for the original artwork would cover his twelve-dollar meal. It was…well, at first it was how he left but then…"

I sat back, ankle on knee, and took a bite off my

burger. Juicy and cooked perfectly rare. I chewed and swallowed and fell into a long think. I'd not seen that kind of a reaction from a person in a long, long time. It took me back to when I'd been stationed at Pearl Harbor-Hickam during my four years in the Navy, fresh after enlisting in high school. Trying not to think of Akumu and the wild first love that had ended so badly, I forced myself to skip by my former lover's memories and focus on his sister. Sweet, tiny Haunani who had a husband who liked to pound on her mentally and physically. Her dark eyes had the same kind of lifelessness Bryan's had.

"Well, I think he sounds like a dick, even if he is hot as sin," Jess stated, then shoved more chicken into her mouth.

I let the subject drop because Jess hadn't seen the young man's expression when I'd begun telling him off. He'd bolted out of fear. He'd flung that arm up in dread. Terror of being struck or berated. I'd bet next month's income on it. But what, or who, on earth could a big, rugged kid like Bryan Delaney be afraid of?

TIME PASSED without a peep from the hockey world. I was buried in work, which was great, and I will never complain about being busy. Well, okay, I will, but I know I shouldn't. I had called Woody in to take a night, so I could skip out early to attend the first preseason game for the Railers. I did have season tickets so why not? Also, it would give me time to check out the new goalie as the teams switched tenders midway through most of the preseason games. When it was time to start the season properly, then Stan would play the last game or two all the way through, but for now, each goalie would get thirty minutes in net. I was keen on studying Bryan. He'd haunted my thoughts since that failed dinner. I wanted to see him again. In the net. I was not there to ogle or drool, although the young man was surely worthy of some saliva. My interest was purely as a fan of the sport. Or so I kept telling myself.

"I wish you'd think more strongly on investing some of your money into CDs," Garrett droned on. He was on his monthly visit to my place to try to make me invest in this or that promotion at the bank making me edgy about missing puck drop.

"Right. Will do," I said as I pulled my Tennant Rowe jersey on.

"Will do, when?"

I tugged to get the collar over my head, then gave my older brother a dark look. He pretended not to see my glare.

"When I have time." The search for my glasses began. I found them on the bookshelf, with no help from Garrett.

"Which will be when?"

Ugh. I swear he was the biggest pain in the ass. Did I look as if I might be in the mood to talk about interest rates, retirement or portfolios? No. I was ready for hockey.

"When you let me give you that first tattoo," I countered, shoved my phone and glasses into various pockets, checked for my wallet and my ticket, and then stared right at my sibling. He had aged nicely. You'd never know he had ten years on me.

"Bankers don't get tattoos." He shut his briefcase with a snap.

"Get one where only Marissa can see it," I teased, knowing his wife would file for divorce if he ever came home with a tat. They were a fine, upstanding, well-to-do couple who had been somehow cursed with a daughter who seemed to be somewhat fluid in her sexual tastes and a brother-in-law who sucked dick, inked people up, and listened to *GASP!* Heavy metal. Which explained why I'd not laid eyes on my sister-in-law for over three years. The sight of me would've induced a massive migraine or some other such bullshit. She played up her distaste well. I had to give the brittle old cow that.

"Yes, of course, I'll jot that down in my day planner. Get a fish tattoo on my balls, Tuesday at one." Garrett sniffed.

I chuckled. The man was wickedly funny in a sarcastic way that really flared to brilliance in my presence. We'd always been like this, even as kids. It was only Gina, our baby sister, who'd been able to buff off the sharp edges of our battles. "Feel free to fritter away your cash then." He pulled on a coat, a rather nice one, long and woolen, and gave me his patented flat look.

"Speaking of which, I have a hockey game to attend. Can I escort you out?" I waved elegantly at the doorway.

"I know the way. I want to stop and pass along a message from Marissa to our daughter."

He never even made the snide remark about spending money on stupid things like hockey tickets or concert tickets or gay porn. What a disappointment. I'd had something all snarky lined up for his hockey jibe.

"Right, well, it was nice to see you. Tell your wife I said hello," I called while sneaking around him and jogging to the front desk. "He's got a message," I whispered to Jess. She rolled her eyes, and I left before I got dragged into some sort of familial thing. I had a game to attend.

It took just ten minutes after hopping on the CAT bus to reach the arena. Driving the short distance was foolish, and my car was at the tire shop anyway. Turnout at preseason games was ordinarily light, so I was pretty much alone in my seat, five rows up from the home bench. I settled in, beer in one hand, a hot dog with lots of mustard and relish in the other, for a kind of pointless game between the Railers and the Devils. I sipped, and I ate, and I relaxed. There were quite a few names from the Carlisle Rush wearing the dusky blue tonight. Maybe some young nobody would make the final cut and be on the team come October. Or perhaps they'd all be sent back down.

Stan was doing an excellent job in net. He seemed to be a little rusty, even though he and the rest of the team had worked all summer to come back to camp firm and ready to play. I looked down at my little belly and sighed. Listen to me talking about others staying in shape. Where had that rock-hard body the Navy had given me gone?

Try a few less beers, hot dogs, and burgers with fries, Gatlin.

"Shut the fuck up self," I grumbled, thankful that the seats around me were empty. The first period slogged past, the veterans putting in time, working out the kinks. Now, the young bucks from the Rush, they were hitting it hard, trying to impress the coaching staff with their wicked mad skills. And then there was Tennant Rowe, my hero. I'd had the pleasure of meeting most of the team since they came to me for all their ink as well as their masks. Tennant was one hell of a good kid, smart, personable, giving and talented. He was my hero because of his strength in coming out as gay in a world that was not always welcoming to gay men. He'd braved it with his man at his side. That took guts. He was still feeling the heat as the country seemed less inclined to be accepting.

So yeah, I admired the kid. And he was a phenom, no way around it. Even now, in the first preseason game when the others were dicking around, Tennant Rowe was determination personified. He snuck a fast shot past the Devils' goalie quicker than I could blink. The scattered fans in attendance hooted, the red goal light flashed, and the Railers goal song played.

That goal was about all the excitement we got until the

goalie change. Then I perked up a bit, which was nothing I wanted to dwell on. Bryan and Stan bumped gloves as they passed each other. My beer was gone, and I really wanted another one, but the need to watch Bryan in net and the small voice in my head whispering about my tiny gut kept me in my seat.

It was interesting to see Bryan working. He seemed focused, tight on the game, his moves quick and sure. He wasn't particularly flashy, but he was sharp-eyed, and his glove hand was a thing of beauty. He robbed one of the Devils' players with a flick of his wrist. That save, seen a moment later up on the Jumbotron, should make the high-light reels. Bryan was pure reflexes. I could tell in the way he moved as if his body were linked to the puck and how it was going to fly at him. The rest of the game rushed by. I was shocked when the rink announcer called out the final minute of play warning.

Bryan was treated to a round of head taps and pats on the back from his new teammates after the final buzzer. He tugged off what was a damn ugly mask. His dark hair was soaked, flat to his skull, and his face was shiny with sweat. He shook his head like a dog, and then he smiled. I'd never seen a smile quite as brilliant. It ignited something inside me, a tiny little ember of undeniable want that I'd thought Rex had permanently snuffed out. I had this insane urge to make Bryan Delaney smile again somehow.

FIVE

Bryan

_____

We'd won! I was on a high, and I couldn't wait to tell Aarni about my success, albeit only in the final half of the game. I wrote and sent a text before I even thought to check how the Raptors had done tonight, and I knew better.

Jesus kid. It's preseason. Doesn't count, idiot. LOL was Aarni's reply. When I checked the scores on the NHL app, I saw the Raptors preseason game against the Kings had ended in a six-one loss for the Raptors.

Shit.

What did I say now? Should I text back and say I was sorry they'd lost? There in Harrisburg I was so far removed from what was happening with the Raptors.

I should have checked.

It seemed to me I'd done nothing the past few days but piss people off. What had happened with Gatlin had guilt pinching at me, and I hadn't been able to shake it all day. The only time I could forget about my rudeness, my melt-down, was when I'd been playing tonight. When I considered how I'd pissed Aarni, and also Gatlin, I was so damn angry at myself.

Gatlin hadn't shouted at me, but the disappointment in his expression and the fact he'd called me on my rudeness had served to give me a very restless night and a thoughtful day.

I typed out a sorry to Aarni, and a sad face, but didn't send it. Was that the right thing to say? It might look like I was gloating, and Aarni was right, it was a preseason game, a way to shake out the kinks after the summer break. It wasn't as if it was important or anything. I deleted the text.

Maybe I could type that I'd been joking; maybe add my own LOL to take the sting out of my obvious crass celebration? I realized I was gripping the phone too tightly, and I willed each muscle to relax. If I cracked another phone screen, that would be seven phones I'd ruined.

As Aarni said, I didn't know my own strength.

Someone toed my foot, and I looked up in surprise.

"You waiting for your girlfriend to call?" Connor asked me. The captain was flushed with heat and wrapped only in a towel, he was intimidatingly gorgeous and toned, standing right in front of me.

"Boyfriend, and no," I said before I even had time to think about lying or bending the truth. The words hung in the air.

Connor's mouth fell open, and then he said in a somewhat high and squeaky voice, "boyfriend?"

My heart sank. I thought the Railers were inclusive. What about Ten? Aarni was right. It was probably one rule for him, and another for everyone else.

Connor shook his head as if he was clearing cobwebs. "Ten," he called.

"Cap?" Ten replied quickly.

"Get over here. Adler, you as well. Stan, Erik, Dieter, fuck…all of you get the fuck over here *now*."

I couldn't understand what was going on. Was this some kind of new-boy hazing? I was trapped in my cubicle, Connor looming over me, his hands on his hips, the towel thankfully staying put, and he'd called over players.

"What's wrong?" I asked.

Erik was the first to arrive, his blond curls wet and flattened. Stan wasn't too far behind him, taller than Erik and peering down at me. He wrinkled his nose in thought and then nodded as if just staring was enough for him to have some sort of epiphany. Dieter sauntered toward me as if he had all the time in the world and quirked a smile when Connor scowled at him. Ten scurried over, his dark hair in soft spikes, and he searched the faces of the small group and looked at us expectantly.

"Wassup?" He continued to button his soft, blue shirt.

Connor appeared to be waiting for something, Adler I guess, and when Adler didn't arrive right away, Connor sighed.

"Ads, get your ass over here now."

"Don't tell me. Someone has killed the new goalie," Adler said from behind the group, then shoved his way to the front. "Oh," he said when he could see me. "Nope, he's alive. That's cool because let's face it, he's better than Jezza with all that Swedish meatball and IKEA shit."

Erik thumped Adler's arm and cursed at him in, what I assumed was, Swedish. It didn't seem as if Adler cared what Erik had said, or maybe he just didn't understand.

I cared a *lot* about what everyone said. I cared that there was a whole fucking group of hockey players surrounding me, blocking me in, looming over me. My chest tightened, my palms sweaty, and I gripped the blocker in my lap, ready to use it as a weapon. Aarni would have come over, pulled them away after a while, made a stand for me, laughed off what they were doing as nothing. Anything to diffuse the situation.

I need Aarni.

What the hell was I doing in this organization? Who thought I was good enough to play on a championship team? I'd done okay today, maybe more than okay, I'd been on a high, and now I'd sunk so low. I waited for the words from the guys in front of me that would shake my confidence.

Connor pointed at me. "He's waiting for a call from his boyfriend." Then he clapped a hand on my shoulder, and I couldn't help it, I jumped. He settled me with a pat. "Welcome to the Railers team, the alternative Railers team, where you have to wear rainbow boxers and like show tunes."

"I don't like show tunes," Adler defended and, this time got an elbow in his side from Dieter.

"What is boxers?" Stan asked. Erik hushed him.

"Is your boyfriend a hockey player?" Ten asked without malice and with real interest. As if I was going to out Aarni to the one man he hated.

I glanced up at all of them in turn and then back to Connor.

"It's a joke, dude," Connor said after a moment of awkward silence. "I just...shit... Ten, I did this wrong." Then Connor sank to a crouch before me and held out a hand to shake, which I took, still utterly convinced I was about to get harassed. "My bad. I'm so used to the same-sex thing now, but I might have channeled too much Adler and ended up sounding like an ass."

"Hey, I resent that," Adler said without heat.

Connor held my hand tightly, and I tried to suppress

the instinct to yank mine away. Something was happening here, but it wasn't cruel; it was just…weird.

"Bryan, you know about Ten, but I promise you the Railers are inclusive. Yeah, we take some heat from fans and visiting teams. It's worse when we play away in some of the less than stellar arenas. It's not easy. In fact, it's fucking hard, but we're a great team, and we can close ranks with the best of them. I wouldn't want anyone else playing alongside me. The Railers are my best friends, and all of us will willingly take any shit thrown at us as a team."

"Always team," Stan reinforced dramatically.

Adler made a show of playing the worlds tiniest violin, and now it was Ten's turn to shove him and shush him. Adler really was an idiot. Cute, a brilliant player, but mostly an idiot who couldn't keep his mouth from running off. I liked him. At least he said what was on his mind, and I could handle things I understood at face value.

"Okay?" I said. Because Connor was waiting for me to say something. He released my hand and grinned up at me.

"You're one of the Railers now, and if you need anything, then you reach out to us. Any of us, rainbow boxers or not. We're a team. Okay?"

"Team. Best," Stan added, and everyone nodded, including me.

"Thank you," I murmured and pushed back my shoulders. I'd heard lip service like this before, but it had always soured a few weeks in. Still, if these guys around me were advocates, then I could count on not being alone, at least for a while. Until I somehow fucked it all up.

"Right. Is the weekly meeting of the Unicorn and Rainbows group over?" Adler asked and sighed noisily.

Connor rounded on him, although he wasn't angry, he

did shove at Adler. Seemed like everyone wanted to push Adler, but in a good way. If that made any sense at all.

"Adler." Connor sniffed the air around him dramatically. "You stink, man."

Adler flicked a towel at Connor and then walked into the shower, leaving a trail of uniform behind him.

The group disbanded, all apart from Ten, who sat in the cubicle two spaces from me.

"Adler means well," he said and looked down to button the rest of his shirt, sighing as he saw he'd buttoned it wrong and undid what he'd done already. "What Connor said, though? You need anything, to talk, or a coffee, or ways to deal with some of the chanting we get thrown at us? You can ask me or anyone." He held up a fist, and after a small hesitation, I made a fist of my own hand and bumped him back.

"Thank you," I said, and I meant it.

I showered and lingered in front of the mirrors pretending to mess with my hair. I needed to think, and that meant not being surrounded by people who wanted to talk to me or reassure me. Not when I had Aarni's newest text front and center in my head. I'd sent him a sad face and simple *yeah, you're right*. The game *had* only been a preseason game. The points didn't matter. Getting so damn excited was silly. Hell, I'd only played thirty minutes.

He'd just sent me a *later, going out, beers*. Did that mean beers as a team? I doubted it. The team was fractured. It probably meant beers with the blonde in the photo.

A hand landed on my shoulder, and I froze, meeting Alain Gagnon's serious gaze in the mirror. The goalie coach smiled when our eyes met.

"Good minutes in net," he said. "Nicely done. Think we need to work on the five-hole, but hell, son, for a young goalie dragged up in a shit team like the Raptors, that was a great start."

I wanted to resent the term *'shit team'*, but I couldn't, not when it was mostly correct. The pride that washed over me at his words was overwhelming. I respected Coach Gagnon, had grown up idolizing him and the goalies of his era fifteen years earlier, wanting to be them despite what anyone else had wanted for me.

"Thank you." It seemed as though I was saying that a lot at the moment.

"Keep it up, Bryan. For practice tomorrow, get here a couple of hours early, and we'll work on some mindfulness. That is if we can pin Stan down. You ever used that?"

I knew what it was, a kind of state where you were aware of yourself or at least something similar. I think when I was in goal I achieved a sort of mindfulness, but whether that was true or not, it didn't matter. I wanted to learn everything.

"Some. I'd like to know more, and I'll be there."

"Good." He left me to finish getting dressed.

I was the last to leave the arena, the city brightly lit around me, the sound of sirens in the distance the only thing I could hear. Mine was the last car, looking all kinds of forlorn sitting in its designated space. The preseason game had been early, a matinee game, and it was only eight twenty-nine. I was sure the tattoo place was open until nine on Sundays, but could I remember how to get there?

I searched on Google and found the place, a logo of a skull two arrows and the name Hard Score Ink. The name alone intrigued me. Was it a play on Hard Core Kink? Or was it referring to the score in a hockey game? Who knew?

You should ask him. What's the worst he can do if someone asks him a question?

I parked outside the shop, a lot closer than I had managed the day before and saw I had only five minutes until the shop closed. The inside was brightly lit, the logo and designs in the window a haphazard display of both color and black-and-gray art.

Channeling the positivity from Coach Gagnon's praise and the offers of friendship from several members of the team, I got out of the car. The walk to the shop was no more than twenty paces, and when I pushed the door open, a chime sounded to indicate a customer. The scrape of metal on the floor was followed by the appearance of someone skidding from behind one of the screens, which hid the workspaces. My breath caught. Gatlin. He blinked at me as if he couldn't believe I was here.

"Can I help you?" he asked with curiosity in his voice.

"I can wait."

Gatlin opened his mouth, probably to remind me of the closing time, but then he offered a small smile and a nod instead.

"Take a seat I'm just finishing up."

I chose the seat nearest to the window from which I was able to watch the road outside and the comings and goings at the bar in front. The sign outside advertised a Railers burger, whatever the hell that was, but I imagined it was something I might like. *I should have one.*

My stomach rumbled, and I pressed a hand there, lost in thought and only shaken out of it when the chime sounded, and I realized the client that Gatlin had been dealing with had left the shop. Gatlin vanished behind the screen again, and I wasn't sure what I should do at that point. Stay and wait or see what he was doing? I decided to cut to the chase and walked around to find him. He was cleaning instruments, putting them into containers filled with blue liquid. When he moved to cap inks, I had to speak.

"I apologize," I blurted out. "For what happened. It was a bad day."

He threw me a look that spoke volumes and then smiled again. "No worries," he said. "You here to talk about your design?"

I backed away. That wasn't what I'd come for, no. It was just to apologize. That's all.

"No, we can make an appointment. Sorry to bother you—"

"You hungry right now?"

No was on the tip of my tongue, but I was hungry, and it was stupid to say otherwise.

"Yes."

"Let's lock up and get a burger. They have the Railers special on tonight; it's always available on game day." He cradled my elbow and squeezed, and there was so much sincerity in his gaze. "Congrats on the win. As a fan, I want to say how cool it is to have a viable backup for Stan. Some people say preseason is a waste, but to see the team come together and try out the rookies, it's a good solid win to have."

I must have flushed scarlet because he chuckled and squeezed my elbow again. He checked the shop, turned off most of the lights except the spotlights that showcased designs in the window and then pulled down the shutters. We left the shop by the back door and walked the small alley to the road, then straight over into Binky's Pub.

The same waitress as before, Tina, showed us to a seat and filled water glasses.

"Two Railers specials?" she asked with a wink.

I nodded as enthusiastically as a man could when not knowing what was in a Railers special.

Only when she left did I lean over to Gatlin. "What is a Railers special?"

"It's a normal burger, all the trimmings, but with special Railers sauce."

I considered my next question so as not to appear too stupid. "And the sauce is?"

Gatlin shrugged, then smiled at me. "Who the hell knows, but it's good."

I took a sip of the water and set down the glass, picking up the fork at my table setting and twirling it in my hands.

"So, I assume you want to talk design?" Gatlin asked and pulled out the notebook from the backpack I'd seen him collect as we left the shop. He pulled his glasses out of the worn blue bag, put them on, and turned to another clean page and sketched the simple helmet shape again, then stared at me expectantly. "Where do you want to start?"

"I don't know." At least I was honest.

He tapped his pencil on the pad, and he had this weird expression, almost as if he could see right through me. I was lost in his gaze, in the way he smiled and it reached his eyes. I knew he was older than me. But by how much? The gray in his neat beard could've indicated any age, and the dexterous way he tapped the pencil like a drumstick made me focus on his hands and the short nails, along with the tail of a design peeking under his red t-shirt. The same shirt that molded to the lean, spare shape of him and made me want to reach over and—

"Tell me why you wanted to be a goalie." He interrupted my thought process, and I mentally shook my head to clear my thoughts.

At this point could I be honest? The real reason why I was a goalie, right back from the start? I'd been frantic to get on the local team way before I came out to my birth parents. Team positions meant practices and games where you needed to travel on a bus to get to them. Being on the local team, even though I was only seven, gave me a reason not to be at home, and I needed that more desperately than I needed air. None of the local players wanted to be the goalie, and at the age of eight, that is what I'd decided I would be. It meant I had a place on the team, and go figure, I was actually pretty damn good. I was also a competent skater even then, and that would hold me in good stead.

I wasn't completely honest with Gatlin though, and instead, I focused on the technical side of standing in goal.

"I think I may have…or at least, it feels like…" I cleared my throat; thankful Gatlin didn't hurry me. "I think I have an uncanny ability to feel the puck coming right at me."

"Like a singular vision?" Gatlin asked and doodled a shape in the corner of the page. To me, it was a bird of prey. He was so talented.

"An owl," I corrected. "Almost as if I can see even with my eyes shut, in the dark I mean, like an owl, or at least hear." I dipped my gaze at the verbal diarrhea I was generating. "None of this sounds remotely rational, does it?"

"I love it, and your story is one you own," Gatlin murmured, and this time the doodle was even more like an owl. He transferred his attention to the mask and sketched in an eye, pulling out an amber pencil and filling in the space. I'd had a day full of emotion, of offered friendship, and then gentle smiles, and I was lost.

No, actually I was spellbound. Witnessing the image being created, hearing the scratch of the pencil on paper, but most of all, studying the arch of his brow, the softness of his skin, and the pink of his lips, that I really wanted to taste. I never wanted to stop watching him.

What?

SIX

Gatlin

B irds of prey were one of my favorite things to draw. Not sure why. Perhaps it was the beauty of their feathers or the gleam in those hunter's eyes. Owls were especially interesting, and this one I envisaged as being a bit steampunk, perhaps. Maybe I could jibe the beauty of the nocturnal hunter with the power and steel of the Railers.

"Food's here."

I glanced up from my sketchpad. Bryan nodded at Tina, who held our platters.

"Sorry," I gave them both a sheepish smile and shoved my sketchpad back into my old backpack. Tina placed our burgers in front of us and refilled our water. I pushed my glasses onto the top of my head. "I kind of get into the zone when I'm creating. Must be like that for you when you're on the ice and your raptor vision kicks in."

His dark eyes widened a bit. "Raptor vision. That's pretty cool."

"There's a video game called *Assassin's Creed* where the main characters have this special skill where they have the sight of an eagle, sort of." I took the top bun off my burger and salted the hell out of the cheese-covered patty. The Railers sauce dripped off the bun, and my stomach rumbled. "The character's sight sharpens when you're in this mode, I guess you'd call it. The player's enemies are easier to pick out. Is your puck sense like that?"

He picked up a lone French fry and dabbed it into the sauce oozing from his burger. "I guess, not really but sort of."

"That certainly clears it up," I joked as I replaced the top bun.

"Sorry, I should speak more concisely."

I looked up from my fries, which I was also salting. Salt is good despite what my doctor says about it and my creepy blood pressure.

"Bryan, you don't have to apologize. I was kidding. Sometimes, we just don't have a straightforward way to describe something spiritual."

He nodded, ate his fry, and then began to retreat into that odd shell he seemed to spend so much time in. I did not want that to happen again. I'd felt him starting to loosen up a bit, and I liked him relaxed. His eyes weren't so sad, his expression not as guarded.

"So, what do you think about a radical steampunk owl on your helmet?" I picked up my burger with both hands and took a huge bite, ensuring he had time to plot out his reply.

"Like, she would be kind of robotic?" He took a bite of his burger as well, and his face softened as ones does when one's mouth is filled with glory.

"Good, huh?" I asked around my mouthful of perfectly flame-broiled beef.

"Super good," he mumbled, then smiled weakly at me.

Oh yeah, there it was. There was that smile. Kind of

puny, but it was there. Now if I could somehow get another one, a less fragile one. One like I'd seen on the ice when he'd been surrounded by his new team.

"Well, a bit yeah. Steampunk is generally steam-powered machinery. I think we could really have fun with this design if you're willing to give it a go?"

He took another bite and chewed lazily. His jaw was strong and covered with a new beard. Lord, but he was a pretty man. So young, so timid, so appealing in so many ways.

He's also as old as your niece or damn close. Which means he could be the same age as your own child if you had one.

No. No. Garrett is ten years older than me. Age is just a number. Fucking hell. In the gay community, it's common for younger and older men to date. So stuff it, inner voice. And we're not dating. We're not even flirting. We're just doing a business dinner. Fuck you.

Right. So you weren't just admiring his jaw and that smooth, supple skin covering his neck? You do that with all your customers? Chickenhawk.

"Are you okay?"

I blinked back into the here and now. "Sorry, I was thinking about your helmet."

He seemed to buy that lie. "Oh, okay. I think I'd like to see what you can come up with for a steampunk owl design."

I smiled widely at him and got a grin in return. Oh hell. My God, he was gorgeous when the shadows left his eyes. What a stunning man. My stomach knotted as I stared at him, willing him to keep smiling. Of course, he couldn't sit there grinning like a fool all night.

We did manage to talk, though, of things other than hockey that made him less rigid in his chair. By the time we'd polished off our food and were contemplating dessert —fine I was the one contemplating—Bryan was close to downright relaxed. His gaze lingered on me as we talked, mostly about my past, since he seemed unwilling to talk about much unless it was music or hockey.

"You sure you don't want some ice cream or something?" I asked while trying to decide on what decadence to indulge in.

"No, thanks. The burger and fries were heavy enough. I'm going to have to put extra time in on the treadmill tomorrow to burn off all those empty calories."

"Yeah me too." I furtively checked out my stomach, then tossed the dessert menu to the table. "Tina? Check, please."

We ambled out into the night, Bryan chattering away about an old KISS album he used to own. I turned to catch his eye.

"You're talking about *KISS Alive*. I have it, on vinyl, signed by Gene Simmons." I looked left and right and then leaned in close enough to be able to pick up the woody scent of his soap. "I might have been a member of the KISS army since…" I coughed into my hand.

He laughed softly, the sound as beautiful as his smile had been visually stunning. "That long huh?"

"Yep. We can go to my place and give it a listen."

And there it was, the first move from me to turn this business meal into something entirely unprofessional. Maybe I should've retracted that invitation. I mean, I never invited Stan up to my place above Hard Score to listen to my scratchy old records. Yeah, this was probably not a good—

His phone rang. "I have to take this. Hold on." He held up a finger, then turned from me, his phone to his left ear. I nodded and waited, grateful for the call because I'd been about to cross a line that I shouldn't. Probably. *Should I? No. Why not?*

Bryan spun to look at me, his face now tight and dark. "I think we should go to your place and listen to KISS."

"Oh okay, fine." I motioned him to cross the street. I walked at his side. All the softness and good humor that I'd been seeing had gone. His jaw was set again, his gaze on the ground, and his shoulders were up by his ears. "We just have to go around back."

I led him to the stairs at the back of Hard Score. I went up first, not saying a word, Bryan's heavy footfalls following mine as they bounced down the alley. The door opened with a soft purr of rusty hinges, and I reached around to flick on the light. It was a small place, homey enough, thanks to Jess and her affinity for painting everything she could slap a brush over. The walls were honey yellow, the large round area rug bright red, and the furniture shades of blue and green.

"This is colorful," Bryan said as he stood in the doorway.

"Jess, my niece, likes to throw color onto everything. Come on in." I tugged off my backpack and jacket, tossed them to the table behind the sofa, and walked to the shelving unit that held a ton of books and my stereo system.

He slowly entered my apartment, closing the door softly as if he feared waking someone. There was nothing below us but an empty tattoo shop. His edginess worried me. I wished he would open up a bit; maybe talk about the issues that had made him so wary, but I doubted he would. Not tonight anyway. But perhaps someday down the road a bit…

"So, take off your coat and join me," I called, pulling out a long drawer on the bottom of the custom-made bookshelf, a trade from a skilled carpenter for a full-sleeve tattoo, then waving at the massive record collection.

Bryan did as asked and then knelt down beside me to flip through the classic rock albums. He had long fingers. They flicked each album gently. He paused at the KISS albums and tenderly lifted my copy of the live double album released way back in nineteen seventy-five.

"How did you get Gene Simmons to sign this?" he asked in a hushed sort of reverent tone that I loved. You could tell the kid was awed by the autograph of a heavy metal demon god of thunder.

"That's a long story. Want a beer?"

He nodded, so I stood, lifted the album from his hands, and pulled one big disc out. Within a moment we were up to our metal-loving ears in *Deuce* recorded live. I ambled off to find a couple of beers in the fridge. When I returned to the living room, Bryan was standing by the record player, eyes closed, lost in the utter bliss of Ace Frehley's guitar riffs.

"They're amazing," Bryan said when I tapped his elbow with a cold bottle of Miller.

"They're damn good. Want to sit down?" I waved my beer at the sofa. He inclined his head, the stress lines around his mouth a little less pronounced. He didn't move though, stood there, cold beer in hand, staring at me as if I had a starfish dancing the Macarena on top of my head. "We can sit down," I offered once more.

He said nothing, only leaned in and pressed his mouth to mine.

To say I was shocked would have been the understatement of the year. I blinked and let him do what he wished to do because I wasn't that shocked that I was going to push him away. His eyes shut. He applied more pressure, his breath warm as it fluttered over my cheek. The drums and bass guitars folded into white noise as the kiss lingered, his lips soft against mine. Then I opened my mouth wide enough to flick at his bottom lip with my tongue. A low growl in his throat told me that he was into this, so I did it again. Maybe, in retrospect, I should have pulled back and asked why he was kissing me. Maybe, be a good man about this instead of a horndog.

But no, I let my stiff dick lead the show. I lapped at his lips wantonly and touched him on the side. Just a touch. Not a lecherous grab, a mere fluttery pass of my fingertips over his ribs. He jerked back violently, his beer sliding out of his fingers and falling to the floor.

"I can't…" He pushed by me and left in such a rush he was out the door before I could think right.

Again, I pounded after him, but this time, he was gone. I sat on the bottom step leading up to my place and stared at the empty alley. A cat crossed a few minutes later, his dark coat sleek and sexy in the flickering light of a streetlamp.

"What the fucking hell?" I asked the stray cat. He leaped onto the lid of a trash can that belonged to the occult bookshop next door and stared at me with golden eyes. "If you're a familiar or something, can you give me some help? Maybe some magical powers that will ensure that my cock does not lead my actions?"

The cat started licking his balls. Nice.

There's your sign, stupid.

"If I could do that, I wouldn't need a man in my bed." I sighed, pushed to my feet, and climbed back to my apartment to mop up beer and ponder on what it was I was getting myself into and why. The why was obvious. Bryan had begun to worm his way into my flesh and, to an extent, into my heart. He was wounded, that was obvious, and I wanted to be the one to heal him if I could. That smile of his should've been seen hourly by the world at large. The what, though? There, I was stepping into was a cloudy mass of uncertainty. While I had a few ideas, I had nothing concrete and so would have to wait until the beautiful yet jumpy goalie came back for his coat. Or I could take it to him tomorrow?

Or you could go take a cold shower and let the man be.

Right. Yeah, that made sense because if I went after him too soon, he'd just balk again. So, I turned off Paul, Gene, Ace, and Peter and got into the shower. I nearly leaped out of my skin when the rushing cold water hit my balls, but it served its purpose. Climbing into my big king-sized bed alone sucked. I threw the spare pillow around, punched it and then tucked it into my belly and spooned it. As I used to spoon Rex. Before I became the equivalent of a Schnauzer in his eyes. The fucker.

Tossing and turning, I played out this Bryan thing. I resolved to never see the kid again. Then I vowed I would try my best to help him out of the dangerous situation I feared he was in. Then I called myself an ass-carrot and rolled to my belly. And then, around two-thirty, I slid out of my tangled bed, pulled on some sleep pants and an old t-shirt, and went out to sip on a beer and listen to Yes. Their *Fragile* album seemed to fit my restless mood as well as it fit the tender young man I was slowly finding myself falling for. My eyes got heavy as I let the music seep into me.

Sleep finally took me around three, and thankfully I got to sleep until eleven or so since my shop opened later in the day. Even with the sleep, I was haggard. I mean, I was no spring chicken, but I looked even older than usual, and I felt it. My heart was heavy with worry about a man who did nothing but run away from me whenever we got close. Why did everyone in my life run? I tugged open my door, and there sat the black cat. He hissed and spat, then dashed down the stairs and out of sight.

"Typical," I mumbled, grabbed Bryan's coat from the sofa, and carted myself and the thick parka down to the shop to face the day. I was in no way prepared to face my older brother waiting for me on the run-down sofa in his tight collar and dustless suit. I knew I should never have given him a key to the shop. Did I need this today? "If you're here about banking or retirement, you can shove it all up your prissy ass."

"Thinking about what you plan to do when this shop closes is hardly something I'd call prissy," Garrett mumbled loudly enough to be sure I heard him.

Ugh. I so wanted to throw a tattoo gun at his head just to ruffle his neatly combed hair. Had I even combed mine? Shit. I didn't think I had.

"You look like someone ran over your dog."

"Rough night."

I pushed the privacy screen to the side and walked into my little area of solitude. Oops, not today, because Garrett came in not a second later.

"Is this foul mood over a man?"

I threw a dark look in his general direction, then spun in a circle, wondering where my glasses were. Fuck sake, how did I lose them all the damn time?

"It's not a man," I lied, then paused to squint at Garrett standing by my desk. "Remember when you used to say I had to rescue everything and everyone? Do you still think that's true?"

"Truest words ever spoken by anyone on Earth." I rolled my eyes. "Do you want me to list all the animals you brought home during our childhood or the men that you had to save from themselves or the big cruel world around them? Dare I mention Rex, the not quite fully recovered abuser of alcohol whom you swore you'd save on sheer determination, love, and willpower?"

"Okay, bringing Rex up was totally unnecessary."

"I rest my case, but if you need proof, I do have a list of all the animals." He gave me a quirk of an eyebrow. Chucking that tattoo gun at him sounded better and better with every passing second. "I'm sure we can gather the data for the ruined men list as well given a day or two to remember them all."

"Fuck. You." I reached up to run my fingers through my hair in exasperation and found my glasses. I yanked them off my head and shoved them onto my face. "Okay, so it is a man. A young man, and my God, Garrett, but he is a haunted human being. I can sense something dark hovering around him, but he's just so skittish."

"Gatlin, you really need to get over not being able to save Gina." He laid his hand on my desk; his gaze was pained. "You cannot possibly rescue every human in dire straits."

"This man has *nothing* to do with Gina!"

"Everything you do has to do with Gina," my brother said with a sigh, gave me a clap on the shoulder, and left before we got into another knock-down fight.

The bell over the front door chimed as he left the shop. It filled me with happiness to know he was gone, mostly because the bastard was right about that one point, anyway. Everything I did went back to my baby sister and how it was my fault she died.

SEVEN

Bryan

The tap on my helmet snapped me back to reality so fast I yelped and stumbled backward, shoving at whoever was in my space, then grabbing a jersey and pulling them with me.

"Shit!" the skater shouted.

"Fuck!" I added to the mix and released my hold, skating back a little, then placing my gloved hand over my heart.

Ten was bent at the waist, his stick across his knees, breathing heavily, and I realized I must have lashed out with my blocker and caught him on the chest. *Fuck. Shit. Not Ten.*

I immediately approached him, my hand on his shoulder, and realized we'd attracted a small crowd of guys in the white practice shirts.

"You okay, Hotshot?" Connor asked Ten, stick tapping his ass.

I should've asked Ten that, but I was struck dumb by the sheer stupidity of what I had done.

I'd been so lost in thoughts about the crap fest that my last week had been that I'd drifted into a daydream.

Getting a call from Aarni, just before I'd gone up to listen to music with Gatlin had been what I needed. I felt attracted to Gatlin and hearing Aarni's voice would have stopped me acting on it. But it wasn't Aarni, it was some guy, taking the phone from Aarni and slurring as he told me he was balls deep and did I want pictures? Of course, Aarni had taken the phone back quickly, but he was out of breath and laughing and acting as if it was fucking nothing.

He was wrong. It was *something*.

Anger drove me to kiss Gatlin. Temper mixed with pain and disappointment welled up in me and spilled over, making the worst mistake of my life. Then Gatlin had deepened the kiss and touched me, and Aarni was in my head, saying I was a cocktease, demanding that I leave.

Hell, I'd left so fast there was no way Gatlin could have caught up, even if he'd tried, which he probably hadn't. I was lucky that Aarni saw past the mess of social awkwardness that was me and to the man underneath. I'd scared off every other man from sex or friendship.

But I'd left my damn jacket at Gatlin's. Which meant getting it back. And what about the helmet design? I'd have to meet him again and see the disappointment in Gatlin's eyes that he even had to waste time with an idiot like me.

Cocktease.

"Earth to Bryan. You okay there?" Connor was talking to me, and I snapped back to the here and now.

Adler was chirping Ten, "Jeez superstar, if you can't take a blocker to the face, then how you gonna take a full check to the boards?"

"Fuck you, Lockjaw," Ten said and straightened. I

expected him to lose his temper right then, to tell me what a fucking idiot I was, but all he did was grin and pat his chest. "That's some right hook you got going there, Bry."

I peered down at my blocker hand and held it up.

"Left hook actually," I managed to say, and everyone laughed. Not at me, but *with* me. "Sorry, Ten."

He clapped me on the shoulder. "My bad for creeping up on you."

"You didn't creep. I mean, I was thinking, is all."

"Well, whatever you were thinking about, it was dead serious." The others had skated away, leaving Ten and me alone, and my usual clumsy social skills came to the fore.

"I left my coat at Gatlin's place," I blurted out.

He gave me a look I was familiar with. One of not quite understanding what I meant but being too polite to actually call me on it.

"Okaaaay," he drawled and skated back to the group. "Anyway, you're up."

I hurried over to the net and turned my back on everyone, placing both hands on the net and bowing my head. Thank goodness they would likely put my idiocy down to some weird goalie thing. After all, they were used to Stan. What I needed though, was just a few moments to still my heart's frantic beating and to forget the fact I'd zoned out completely, thinking about things I shouldn't have been thinking about.

I couldn't get the kiss out of my head. Seven days, and I was lusting for another taste of Gatlin or at least another meal at the bar where we could talk music. He'd actually listened to my opinions and seemed to find me interesting until I'd fucked up the whole thing.

Aarni had called me to explain who the stranger was with his phone. A friend over to visit. That was all. The reason was real, and I accepted his regret, all the while consumed with guilt.

Maybe I should just stay away from Gatlin. I had enough money to buy a new coat, and I could find another artist for the helmet.

But I want to see Gatlin.

I owed the man one hell of an apology for forcing myself on him, and my lame explanation text the next morning had gone unanswered. I was still kicking myself over what had happened.

One stupid phone call from Aarni and I'd lost control. Spiraling to become a desperate man who used his height and weight to force a kiss on a man who might not even like men.

You've seen the way he looks at you. You've seen the rainbow tattoo on his wrist. You've felt him touch you in a familiar way.

Tension shot through me, and I felt ill, nausea climbing inside me, and God help me, I thought I was going to be sick.

Someone moved up on my side, and I knew it would be Stan. He'd hovered over me the last few days. We'd played another preseason game against Boston, and I'd blown it so badly I was surprised I still had a contract. Ten minutes on the ice, five shots on the Railers' goal, and every single fucker had gone past me. I was like a sieve out there, and Coach called me off the ice, sending Stan back in.

Mental strength was vital for a goalie, and my raptor-sense had failed spectacularly.

Stan tapped the pipes. "Good pipes, like talk."

I peered into the warm eyes, saw the mask resting on his head, the Railers' logo right there, in gorgeous swirling smoke, Gatlin's work, and something gripped me hard in my chest.

"Touch," Stan ordered and poked at the net, and

instinctively I did as I was told, patting as Stan did and pasting a smile on my face. "Is good in head," he added and then skated back to the opposite end of the rink right up to Coach Gagnon. What was he saying to the goalie coach? Was he explaining that I was fucking up?

I pulled down my face mask and turned to face the team with determination, all of them lined up waiting and chatting and absolutely not staring at their sorry excuse for a backup goalie.

I settled my breathing, leaned over and cleared my thoughts, then bounced in place, bent my knees, and finally, I was ready.

I nodded, and Ten's line was up first, a give and go, passing crisply, and when my hand was there, the glove catching the puck, it was as if I had steel in my spine. Fuck everything else, this is what I loved, and I was good at it. The rest of it was just noise.

The practice ended with me sweating, tired and happy, and we made it back to the dressing rooms, Adler shooting his mouth off about strawberry shampoo and figure skaters or some such nonsense, and Dieter shoving him every so often.

"A word when you're done here," Coach Gagnon said in passing. There was no accusation in his tone. He didn't seem angry, but the feeling of dread that had marked this morning was back with a vengeance.

Showered and dressed, I made my way to the Coach's room, standing aside to let Jared Madsen out, and not quite being able to look him in the eye after what I'd managed to do to Ten. He didn't seem like he wanted to kill me, so that was a good thing.

Maybe he hasn't heard yet.

I rapped on the door frame, and Coach Gagnon, talking and smiling on the phone, gestured me in.

"Shut the door, son," he said. The dread intensified, so it was a dead weight on my chest. "Have a seat."

I took the worn seat and shuffled back from the table so I could fit in the small space left for visitors.

"I can do better," I said quickly. "Sorry about Ten."

He ignored what I said, rested his elbows on the table, steepled his fingers, and regarded me thoughtfully, "How are you, Bryan?"

"Good," I lied. He made a soft noise, a disbelieving *hmmm*, and that wasn't a good sound, particularly when he frowned as well.

"How are you finding the mindfulness sessions?"

I opened my mouth to lie, but he was staring right at me, and I thought he could even see through me. I actually found them impossible because I had to sit in silence and listen to my body, and it wasn't natural. I think I did it already, but not in such a purposeful way.

"Difficult, Coach."

He nodded and smiled softly, and I was relieved that I'd said something right. He paused for a moment, and I wondered if he wanted me to say anything else.

"Okay, here's the thing. I know how hard it is to come from another team, and I'd like you to get some help with settling yourself here. I made an appointment with Mitchell Grafton. He's on-call for the Railers as our therapist for today. He's an ex-skater, a good man, and I'd like you to see him for a chat."

A therapist? Jesus, I'd spent most of my life avoiding that shit, and I scrambled for a reason why I didn't need to talk out my feelings.

"I already apologized for hitting Ten. It was an accident. Wrong place wrong time," I defended.

"Ten has had worse than a blocker to the chest."

"It was an accident. He talked to me, took me by surprise. I was in the zone."

The lie tasted horrible on my tongue, but Alain Gagnon was a former goalie and would know what it was like to be in the zone.

It worked. He chuckled, then coughed to clear his throat. "Okay, so we're looking at an appointment beginning in ten minutes. Make your way up to concourse level, and it's room C twenty-three."

"What? Now?"

"Now."

"But, Coach, I have time booked for strength and conditioning."

"You can make it up."

He looked at me steadily, and I knew I had to say something to make this all go away, but I wasn't about to argue with the man who held my future in his hands. All he had to do was tell our GM or head coach I wasn't mentally fit for this and I was gone from the Railers.

"Bryan?"

I snapped back to Coach's voice. "Sorry?"

"This isn't up for negotiation."

Aarni's chuckle filled my head, *"I knew you wouldn't last a month there."*

"Yes, Coach."

WHICH IS how I found myself standing outside room C twenty-three, hand in a fist, ready to knock, and feeling like a fifteen-year-old kid meeting my billet family for the first time. I knew back then my new family would have so many questions, and it was a familiar dread that gripped me. I stepped back from the door and leaned against the wall, thankful that this room was in a curved corridor with a dead end past it. No reason for anyone to walk past and see how fucked up Bryan Delaney was.

Then, before I could second-guess myself anymore, I rapped on the door and entered at the muffled "Come in".

I expected a couch and a man with gray hair who would stare at me as I cried my way through life.

Instead, there were sofas with cushions and jerseys in glass frames around the room. The pen holder on the desk was a miniature replica of the Stanley Cup, and the man I was there to see was on his hands and knees on the floor, picking up what looked like an entire lifetime's worth of paper clips.

"Shit," he said. "Sorry, I'll be with you in a minute. I didn't have the appointment until half an hour ago, and I was unpacking." He returned to the job in hand and scooped clips into a pile. "Pass me that would you?" He gestured to a cardboard container which had rolled toward the door. I picked it up and passed it to him. He scooped each paperclip in there and finally stood, brushing off his pants, and then extending a hand to me.

"Mitchel Grafton, call me Mitch, and you're Bryan Delaney, the backup goalie. I saw you play against the Jets back in fifteen. Nice saves in the shootout, good hands."

I wasn't expecting a guy who didn't stop talking, but seriously he was all smiles and happy and confident. I hated him and really wanted out of the room.

"Thanks," I said instead.

"Sit, sit." He chose one sofa, so I took the other, easing back into the comfort of dark leather and waiting for the questions to start. "Tell me the truth," Mitch began and leaned forward, all earnest and focused.

Here we go.

"I'll try," I said.

"I read you sometimes close your eyes in practice. Is that for real?"

Wait. Where was the searching question about my parents or my sex life or my opinions on images I could see in ink blots?

"Yes." I cleared my throat. "I know it's strange, but I connect with the ice."

Mitch grinned at me. "That is the coolest thing I've ever heard. I played hockey at college level, not a goalie but as part of the leakiest defense in the NCAA. Maybe we should have all closed our eyes and felt a connection with the ice."

Is he teasing me? Is he laughing at my weirdness?

He didn't seem to be. I couldn't see that he was anything but genuine.

"Maybe," I said.

"Anyway, where do we start? Coach Gagnon wanted me to talk to you about mindfulness, but before we do that, I'd like to get a feel for the real Bryan Delaney. Where were you born?"

I gestured at his lap. "Don't you need a notebook or a file?"

He shook his head, "I don't take notes. I'm not that kind of therapist. I just want to talk, man-to-man, see how we can work together to make your thoughts a little calmer in the net."

"What if I don't need that?"

"We'll work out if you do or not and take it from there."

Resigned and not able to run for the door, I laced my fingers together in my lap, my palms sweaty, my chest tight, and steeled myself for all kinds of searching questions. Starting with where I was born, which would lead to my parents.

"I was born in Canada," I said before he could ask me again. I had this story carefully plotted, and it was all in my bio if you looked hard enough. "My dad was a mechanic; my mom was a secretary for the local Catholic church. I went to school in the town I was born in, played my first hockey game at four with my best friend, Darren, and moved to a billet family in Erie when I was fifteen."

Mitch watched me carefully. "Let's start at the beginning."

Please, let's not.

"Why?"

"I just want to get a better picture."

Irritation spiked. What the hell gave the Railers the right to know anything past my basic information? I was theirs now, but all that stuff from my childhood wasn't important. I even had the words on the tip of my tongue to say just that, but Mitch beat me to it.

"So, your dad was a mechanic; your mom a secretary. Did either of them play hockey?"

I couldn't help the snorted laugh, imagining my sour-faced mother on skates or my dad drunk off his head trying to stand up on dry land, let alone ice. Of course, that was the wrong thing to do as I caught a glint of interest in Mitch's steady gaze.

"How did you get into hockey?"

"My best friend's uncle was a coach and our local priest. He would take us both."

"Priest? Are you a practicing Catholic?"

"No."

That was a can of worms I was *not* opening, and I guess my tone was enough for him to back off. The irritation inside me was acid under my skin, and I had to try damn hard to sit still in the chair.

"You left home at fifteen."

Not a day too soon.

"A lot of hockey kids get selected to play and live with new families."

"I know. Tell me about the family you ended up with."

"Daisy, my billet mom, is married to George, and they have two children of their own, Emma and Tom. I loved my time with them until I moved to Arizona after the draft took me to the Raptors."

"But you weren't happy at home in Canada?"

"I never said that."

Mitch frowned and shook his head. "The Raptors are a hard team." He didn't elaborate, and I wasn't going to give anything away. "Are you still close to your billet family?"

By the time the session had finished, Mitch knew very little about the real me, and I certainly hadn't told him about the first fifteen years of my life or getting caught kissing the priest's nephew or why I wasn't a Catholic anymore. Hell, I hadn't even told him about Aarni being my boyfriend, although I did tell him I was gay. He didn't bat an eyelid at anything I actually deigned to say to him. I was congratulating myself on my success and actually felt calmer, so maybe there was something with this talking business.

"Thank you for coming to see me," Mitch concluded and shook my hand. I'd made it all the way into the hall, heading in the direction of the stairs when he called after me. "Same time Friday?"

I sketched a wave back at him, didn't actually say I'd be there. That was all I could manage right now. I was exhausted from skirting the truth and avoiding the past, and my head hurt.

It didn't help when Ten cornered me by the lockers as I pulled out the thick fleece that had replaced my coat.

"Check your phone. There's an invite on there for a

preseason party at our place. Beer, talking, and I think Jared's doing barbecue."

"I'm not sure I can make it," I blurted and realized what I'd done. He hadn't even mentioned a date, and I had just fucked myself over. The last thing I wanted to do was be social with the team. When the Raptors got together outside hockey, it was an excuse to get drunk and pick on anyone who showed vulnerability. The quiet goalie was at the top of everyone's lists. But don't think for one minute I can't think on my feet. "I'm washing my hair," I quipped and turned the whole thing into a joke.

Ten went from confused to happy in a millisecond, and he fist-bumped me.

"Sunday, starts at four, details on the phone."

He left then, in his cool Railers' jacket, and I looked at my stupid ass Raptors fleece and threw it back into the locker.

I might not be with the Railers very long, but I could get one of the jackets and eBay it later when they dumped my ass.

I had two preseason games to prove I wasn't a fuckup and solidify my place as a legitimate backup to Stan, and one team party to get through without seeming like an idiot.

But all I could think about was Aarni and the blonde or the unidentified man on the phone or Gatlin and his soft voice and kind eyes.

And I was tired of it all.

EIGHT

Gatlin

"You come."

I glanced up at the Russian sitting in my chair, getting some color added to a new tattoo. Stan stared back at me.

"You come."

"Stan, I appreciate the offer, but it's kind of last-minute notice. I might have something planned for that night."

"What plan? You got better plan to party with us?" He stared right into me. I returned my attention to the soft blue going into the small baby bunny on his wrist. A little blue bunny. All fuzzy and adorable with the name of his son inked in among the flowers Noah the bunny was cavorting in. Well, I guess Noah was Erik's son, but try telling Stan that. Or Stan's mother. That boy was theirs as much as he was Erik's.

"I didn't say I had plans. I said I might. You okay?" I glanced up again, pulling the needle from his skin after he had moved his hand. "Getting too intense on the pulse point? Lots of people complain about that. We can take a break."

"No, it good fine for pulse points. I need you tell me you come. Big party. We bring Mama and Noah. Many wife and children. One beer only why hard training for new season. Make good times. You come."

I sighed. "Stan…" It wasn't that I didn't want to go. I did. I loved the guys on the team and was kind of flattered to be thought of as one of their inner circle. But where the Railers were, Bryan was sure to be, and that whole festering mess had yet to be resolved. Why? Oh, because the big bad tattoo artist didn't have the balls to call the man, or vice versa it seemed. That kiss had elevated things from mere attraction to fuck-me-now, and I wasn't sure Bryan was on board with—

"You look goofy-faced."

"I was born looking like this," I quipped to cover my lapse.

Stan chuckled, then flexed his hand to work out the tingling in his fingers, I wagered.

"You sexy old man."

"Thanks." I sniggered, sitting straight to work out the kinks being bent over his arm had brought.

"I no mean old man. Old man like young man but not so old dick no work good no more. See? I make clear sunny day as shine on face!"

I had no idea what he had just said. "Yep, clear as a sunny day on shine face."

"Ah, we speak good talk. You smart man. Smart come with old. So, you come."

I folded my arms over my chest, tattoo gun in my right latex-covered hand. "Are you going to keep pestering me until I give in?"

He nodded strongly. "I pester big much. You come. See friends. Eat good foods. Bounce baby Noah on knee. You come."

"Okay, I give up." I held up my hands. "I'll go. Text me the directions to Tennant and Jared's place."

His grin was wide and sincere. "Is good you come! You see. Big good times for all."

I doubted Sunday night would be filled with big good times, but at least it beat sitting around, staring at Bryan's jacket while I played with myself.

"Now do work on new Noah inks."

"It was you who kept distracting me," I pointed out with a soft laugh.

Stan's smile grew wider. "Yes, but you come now. Distracting make work mighty fine."

SUNDAY NIGHT ARRIVED, and I was pretty sure not much was going to be mighty fine or even a little fine. I felt stupid, underdressed, too damn old, and was about to knock on Jared Madsen's door with Bryan's coat over my arm. Shit. Maybe I should've gone back and thrown it into my car. Yeah, good call. I dashed to my car, chucked the coat in, and then jogged back to Jared's and *then* rang the bell. I could hear the party from out here. When the door was yanked open, the sounds of laughter, both adult and children's, leached into the early October evening.

"Gatlin, dude, so glad you made it!" Tennant grabbed my hand, shook it, and then pulled me into his home. "Yo! Our ink man has arrived."

Everyone in the tastefully decorated apartment greeted me. I lifted a hand, and my sight flew to Bryan standing by an old upright piano. Seeing him sucked the air from my lungs. How was it possible that he'd gotten even better looking since I'd last seen him? That shaky kiss flashed through my mind as we stood drinking each other in while I made small talk with Ten and Jared. They shoved a soda into my hand. Two young boys ran past, one bouncing into and then off Tennant's leg.

"So yeah, I'm working my best charm to get Bryan to join our Pokémon group, but he's holding out hard. Think you could maybe discuss how painless it is to get new ink?"

I gave Tennant a lifted eyebrow. The kid had the grace to look a little shamed.

"Okay, so they do *kind* of hurt, but he's just balking because…well, I don't know why. I know he wants in because, yeah, it's Pokémon, but every time we mention the tattoo part, he gets all ashen and shit."

"Maybe he just doesn't want a tattoo. Not all of us do, Tennant," Jared interjected, his hand lying on the back of Ten's thick neck, right over Rowe's own tattoo.

"Maybe, but I think if he just talked to a professional about it…"

"Okay, I'll go talk to him about tattoos."

"You rock." Ten and I rapped knuckles, and then I meandered toward Bryan. Each step I got delayed by hockey players or their wives, many who had also come to me for ink, until about fifteen minutes later, I finally stepped in front of the man who had been haunting my dreams for days.

"You're popular," Bryan said, holding a can of pineapple soda.

I'd never seen pineapple soda before. "Is that some sort of Canadian thing?" I asked, waving my good old can of Coke at the yellow can in his hand.

"Oh, not that I'm aware of. Stan said it was an American classic."

"Stan's probably not the one to talk to about Americana."

"Probably not." He lifted his gaze from the soda in his

hand. Our gazes met and locked. "I guess you're wondering why I left the other night."

"Nope, I have a pretty good idea why you ran. I scare you."

His pretty eyes flared for a second. Then he exhaled, the sound desperately sad. "Sort of, yeah."

"You kind of scare me too."

His gaze warmed just a bit. The impulse to lean into him and put my mouth on his was huge, and I would have and damn the consequences, were it not for the kids running around with inflatable hockey sticks bearing the Railers steam engine logo.

"I have your coat."

"Yeah, I know."

This was going smoothly. If racing a car off a cliff was smooth.

"Bet you're cold without it."

He shrugged.

I was now torn between wanting to suck on his tongue or shake him like a maraca. Both had merit.

"Gatlin."

"Bryan."

We both blinked at each other after speaking at the same time. I pushed my way into the awkward silence that followed.

"Bryan, how about we finish our drinks and go somewhere to talk. I think we really need to do that."

He nodded slowly but with conviction. I will not say how happy that bob of the head made me. A baby started crying behind me. I glanced over my shoulder to see Stan's Erik trying to soothe their fussy son. Stan rubbed the boy's belly gently, but the tyke was falling into a true screaming fit by the sounds of his increased volume.

"I am think he has sidesaddle fart," Stan announced to the room. Several people, probably parents, giggled, and the rest of us just chortled at Stan. "Or is mad over ugly music on radio. Tennant, find us good baby song."

"Uh, well, I can't just pull kids' music out of the air," Tennant said.

"Play something for the boy. That might soothe his jagged temper," Jared interjected as Noah grew louder. "Ryker always loved people singing to him."

"Right, okay, I can play something. Bring him over here." Tennant wiggled past me. I stepped into a small space on Bryan's left. Our arms rubbed with warm familiarity, and I was thrilled that he didn't jerk away from the friction.

Ten sat on the piano bench, Jared resting his hands on Tennant's broad shoulders. Stan settled on the side of the sofa beside Tennant, Erik lingering behind the big Russian. People began to crowd in. I'd not had a clue that Tennant Rowe knew how to play the piano, although he may have mentioned sheet music for a Panic! At the Disco song during one of his ink sessions.

"I think I have an old book full of Disney songs," Ten was saying as he shuffled through a couple of thick stacks of sheet music.

"It's behind the Bach," Jared pointed out. Ten gave him a flashing smile, then tugged the book out from behind loose sheaves of paper filled with lines and musical notes. It was all Greek to me. I love the hell out of music but can't read a note of it.

"Right, here we go." Ten tapped a key, and Noah sniffled a bit, his screaming coming to a fast halt. Stan dabbed at the lad's round, wet cheeks with a tissue. "Does he like Winnie the Pooh?"

"Yes, he is big liking Pooh and Piglet. Tigger too!" Stan replied, bouncing the boy on his knee.

Several of the older kids wiggled through the adults. Ten smiled at them all and then played. Noah's eyes grew as round as dinner plates, his lower lip stopped trembling. Tennant, with a voice so lovely that it shocked me into stupidity, began singing about going up and down and touching the ground. When another verse started, every parent in that spacious apartment sang along, as were a bunch of kids. Noah was now drooling in glee, his eyes sparkling.

Bryan's knuckles brushed the back of my hand. I glanced to the side and wasn't sure what I saw in his gaze. Surprise maybe, mixed with some other strong emotions. Did he want me to take his hand right here? No, surely not. I replied by tickling his knuckles with my index finger. His lips twitched a bit. I felt a little giddy. Imagine a man of my age and horrific track record with romance feeling giddy over something as simple as a mere brush of flesh against flesh. It was insane. *I* was insane.

When the song concluded, Noah squealed in delight, the partygoers clapped, and Ten let his head drop back to rest on Jared's stomach. Our defensive coach leaned down and kissed his boyfriend so sweetly that I ached inside. Talk about envious.

"Want to go talk now?" Bryan whispered beside my ear.

"Sure."

We kind of faded back through the group of men, women, and kids and slipped outside to make our escape. I took his coat out of the back of my car and handed it to him. He slid his long arms into it, a wobbly smile on his lips.

"Thanks."

"So where do we want to go to talk?"

"I'm sorry about the last time we were together."

Okay. Guess we were talking here. In the parking lot of Jared's somewhat upscale apartment building.

"Me too," I replied. "Bryan, we should maybe take this somewhere less drafty than this parking lot."

He glanced around as if he had forgotten that we were standing outside. "Right, yeah, uhm, your place?"

"Sure." I slid into my car after giving him a self-conscious smile. He followed at a sedate rate. We parked in front of the shop and walked around back, him at my heels, and up the creaky metal stairs. Curled up on the welcome mat was that black cat. He seemed disinclined to move, so I stepped over him after the door was unlocked.

"Should I leave the door open for your cat?" Bryan asked as he sidestepped the cat snoozing on the mat.

"He's not my cat." I shucked off my coat and flung it to my favorite old recliner. I took a deep breath and turned. Bryan was closing the door gently, as if scared he would pinch the slumbering cat. It was quite the endearing sight. And there it was—that stupid, giddy feeling. For fuck's sake. This was moronic. You'd think I'd never been kissed before.

"You want something to drink?"

"No, I don't want to have a sloppy head, and we're going to be opening the season soon." He took his coat off and laid it right where it had lain before. I couldn't help but check him out. His black jeans fit him well, as did the long-sleeved shirt he'd pulled over a soft gray vest. "Are you mad at me?"

"No, not at all. I'm feeling a little ratty, to be honest," I joked, tugging at my favorite sweater, an old rust-toned one that Rex, the prick, had given me. "This is pretty much dressing up for me." An old sweater and worn Levi Strauss. Typical Gatlin.

"You look good. I mean…" He slapped a hand to the back of his neck. "Good, like dressed well for a party. Casual. I always feel like I need to be…uhm, do more."

Shit, this was uncomfortable. Erotic pulses danced between us, but I had no idea how to move on them.

"Let's sit down." There, that was good. Sitting was better than standing. Christ on a cracker I was an idiot.

But we sat after we managed to pick out some music without really looking at each other. We agreed on some Rush before we sat down facing one another.

"You ever see them live?" Bryan asked, settling into the conversation about music smoothly. Chatting about rock bands wasn't exactly what I was hoping to do, but if it put him at ease, I'd talk Rush all night.

"Once, back in the late eighties. I was eight or nine at the time. Garrett, my older brother, was nineteen and took me along. I threw myself all over the place until he agreed to take me. My little sister, Gina, she was just two. She wanted to go as well, but Garrett was *not* taking a toddler to a Rush show. That was my first rock concert. They were phenomenal."

"Did your sister ever get to see them play again? They were touring just a few years ago," he said, impressing me with his knowledge of the rock world.

"No, she uh, she never got to see them."

This time it was me making a move. It was a fumbling, stupid move, filled with a dopey lunge that ended up with us bumping noses. Yes, I was going in for a kiss to divert him from asking why Gina never got to see Rush.

Because I let her die, that's why. Now fucking shut up and kiss me and ease this pain.

He tipped his head, his eyes simmering and hot, then

opened for me when I moved in to try again. I crawled up over him, his tongue roaming around inside my mouth, his hands sliding under my sweater. I rocked into him a bit, my cock gouging him in the belly. He was a lanky man, powerful legs tangling with mine as we 'talked about things'. His kisses made me hot and hard, slewing my thought processes until all I could think of was his skin next to mine from head to toe.

"You're delicious." I panted as we wrestled to get my sweater off and then worked on his vest and shirt. When we were bare from the waist up, he grabbed my head, hands big as dinner plates locking to either side of my skull and leading my mouth back to his. We came up for air a few minutes later. "I mean, like possibly the most entrancing taste to have ever touched my taste buds."

He smiled. Holy hell, that smile lit up the room. No, it probably lit up the whole freaking block.

"I like kissing you." Then he sighed, tugging on my neck until our mouths were fused yet again. I licked deeply, rolling my cock into him, getting a long growl that nearly had me coming in my shorts. That was just not going to happen. Not to a man who could see forty clearly on the horizon.

"We should…shit," I gasped, trying to leave his lips and finding it impossible.

I nuzzled his neck. His fingers worked the flesh on my back, fingertips digging in deep, as I suckled hungrily. A familiar tingle in my balls made me pull back a bit. I sat back on my couch, my lungs working overtime to pull in oxygen. He lay there, back flat to the couch, legs akimbo, lips puffy, and chest working as hard as mine. I placed my hand to his chest, right on his sternum. There was a fine line of dark hair there. It crinkled and tickled my palm.

"Now that we got that out of our systems, we really should talk."

Bryan licked those swollen lips, then inclined his head.

Good. Okay. I'd taken control of things before I embarrassed myself.

"I need a beer."

"Go for it. Got any spring water?"

"Uhm, maybe?" I got up, pushed at the impressive erection trying to bust my zipper, and walked in some discomfort to the kitchen. I had to rummage around to find a bottle of water, but I did and, with something for both of us, went back to sit down beside him.

"It's kiwi-flavored. Jess must have left it here for me. She's big on trying to make me take better care of myself." I handed him the water and twisted the cap on my beer. Bryan was resting comfortably, his back pressed deeply into the cushions.

"Not sure I've ever had a kiwi," he mumbled as I leaned up to rest my elbows on my knees, my beer dangling from my fingers. I needed to think of a way to get him to open up a little.

"No, me either. When did you know you were into classic rock and metal?"

He sipped his water, made a terrible face which made me snicker, and then handed the kiwi water back to me.

"Sorry, but that is rank, and I've had some awful protein drinks before."

"It's fine. I won't tell her. So, metal. Tell me how you found yourself wrapped in its seductive arms."

I leaned back into the couch cushion. Bryan stared at me oddly. "I like how you phrase things. Like calling rock a seductress. It kind of is though, right? I mean, the lyrics are so pure, so brutally true, that you have to give yourself up to them."

"Exactly. Take Rush for example. If you really listen and absorb the words to *Free Will*, for instance, you've got to be—what?"

His mouth was on mine before I could finish my statement about Rush. Kind of a shame because I had an excellent point to make, but for the life of me when his tongue tangled with mine, I could not recall what that good point had been.

This time, he pressed his weight into me, pushing me back into and over the arm of the couch, his leg easing between mine. The man was one hell of a kisser. Hungry. Ravenous even. The ridge of his cock rocked into my hip. Both of us sucked in a sharp breath through our noses because we didn't dare break apart long enough to breathe properly. I wanted him in ways that I'd not wanted a man in…maybe ever. I rubbed my hands over his arms, loving the ebb and flow of his biceps as he thrust that long, hard dick of his against me. My own cock was rigid as well. This petting and humping was fun, but after a few long strokes of my tongue over his, we needed to step this up or call it a night.

I made a move and shoved my hand between us, searching for his fly, the pressure of his erection against my palm making me groan into his mouth. With a flick of his hips, I found the zipper and tugged it down. The impatient thing that I am, I crammed my hand into his pants, finding the band of his briefs, then slipping under the material. I brushed the head of his cock. A slick trail of pre-cum dampened my knuckles as I searched for the base of his prick. No sooner had I wrapped my fingers around him than he tensed.

Cursing inwardly, I released him, and he rolled off me to one knee, and then awkwardly he pushed to his feet. Lying there hard as a new two-by-six, short of breath, my balls heavy with want, I looked at him standing by the end of the sofa and wondered if he were getting ready to run yet again. I held his gaze, then slowly got to my feet and walked to him, reaching for him, my fingers running up his neck and then around to cup his skull. I was not going to let him make a dash without trying one last time to tempt him to stay with me. He leaned in for the kiss, and I made damn sure it was one of my best kisses ever.

NINE

Bryan

W hen we parted, it wasn't only me who'd been affected by the kisses. Gatlin was flushed, and he smiled at me, and then he leaned in for more.

And all I could think was what the hell had I done. I was in a relationship, and I'd kissed another man. *Jeez, my head is fucked up.*

I was mortified that I'd melted into Gatlin's arms, and remorse at leading him on warred with arousal. This kissing and then running was getting tiresome, and I had to explain. I quickly shook off Gatlin's hold and stepped back until my ass hit the table.

"I'm sorry," I didn't have the words to excuse what I was about to say.

Gatlin stepped closer, a smile curving his lips, his gaze soft and his tattoos clear in the light spilling from the kitchen.

I wonder what they all mean? There are so many of them.

I wanted to ask, but that was a level of intimacy I couldn't go into right now. Not until I cleared the air between us. What I felt with Gatlin was explosive, so much more than the hidden sex I'd had with Aarni. Aarni didn't kiss or hug or spend ten minutes tracing the shape of my body. Sex with Aarni was rough and fast, and hurtful and angry, Aarni stamping his authority on me as if that was what sex was about.

And I took it because that was what I thought a relationship was. Aarni was my only frame of reference for what was expected from another man.

Tonight, I hadn't even made it to bed with Gatlin, but I swear I'd felt more in that short time than I had after three years of being *with* Aarni.

"I have a boyfriend," I said and waited for the explosion of anger.

Gatlin stopped prowling toward me. Stopped dead no more than two feet away, his expression morphing from aroused affection to awful understanding.

I closed my eyes, knowing I deserved whatever Gatlin threw at me. Any and all hate and anger from Gatlin was okay with me as long as he felt better about what I'd done.

"Jesus. Okay. Look, these things happen. It's okay," he said.

"No, it's not. I shouldn't have let things get this far." Aarni was right. I was nothing more than a cocktease. I opened my eyes to see that Gatlin hadn't moved an inch. He still looked shocked, but there was no anger there. Instead, there was caution in his gaze, and he was calm, his thumbs hooked into his belt loops.

I hoisted up my open pants, buttoned them, hot tears pricking my eyes. Craving Gatlin's temper was one thing, but all I was seeing was understanding or maybe indifference as if nothing of what we'd done actually mattered enough to waste emotions on.

"I said, it's okay," Gatlin murmured.

"That's what I do, you know. I have this man back in

Arizona, but I still came up here with you, leading you on. Fuck." I dragged a hand through my hair and gripped hard. "You have every right to be angry with me."

"I'm not angry," Gatlin said.

I stiffened at the bewilderment in his tone. "You should be." I tilted my chin up and pushed my shoulders back. "You can be angry with me, say whatever you want. I led you on. I can take it."

Gatlin's gaze narrowed. "I don't know what you're asking for." He remained confused. "Did you kiss me just to try and make me angry when you told me about a boyfriend?"

"No! Yes... Fuck, I don't know."

"I'm not going to lie. I'm thirty-eight years old, and I never thought I'd ever have an attraction to someone as instant as what I feel for you. I'm sad, but this isn't on you. I misread the situation, but I'm a grown man. It's fine." He turned from me and picked up his shirt, slipping it over his head to cover the beautiful angel on his back. "Come on, let's just listen to music and you can tell me about tomorrow night's game. It's the first of the season, and I can't wait to see how the Railers do this year."

I listened to the words, the lack of heightened emotion, the acceptance, and something inside me snapped, my heart aching with the pain of it.

"I can't," I said. "I have to go."

Gatlin reached for me, but I avoided the hold, scrambled to put on my shirt and jacket, and with those damn tears threatening to fall, I went to the door. Gatlin didn't try to stop me, only stood there watching, his expression thoughtful.

"You don't have to go." Gatlin wriggled his hands. "I can keep these to myself." He was apparently trying to ease the tension, but it was all wrong. I needed more; passion and fire and temper.

I'm so fucked up.

"I need an early night." I kept my tone even. "Thank you."

I could feel the weight of Gatlin's gaze from the apartment window as I walked away from the shop.

So, I left crying until I was safe inside my car.

Back in my apartment, I felt torn apart and exposed, and my head spun. I owed it to Aarni to tell him what had happened tonight. How I'd let myself feel something for another man, so I pulled my cell out of my pocket, then stared at it for the longest time.

Finally, I scrolled my contacts and connected to Aarni, who answered on the third ring, just as I'd expected it to go to voicemail.

"Bryan," Aarni shouted over the noise that was behind him. It sounded like a party, probably some kind of preseason thing like they had every year. Only the Raptors let loose in the wildest way, it wasn't like the Railers' party with family and babies and playing the piano. They would have a DJ, and even this close to playing, there would be some players who drank heavily, Aarni included.

"What am I to you?" I shouted so Aarni could hear me over the volume of the party.

"What?" Aarni shouted back.

"What. Am. I. To. You?" I repeated, speaking as loudly and clearly as I could.

Silence from Aarni as a cheer from the people in the room filled my ears. Then the chaos muffled, and I realized Aarni had taken the call somewhere a bit quieter. Knowing Aarni, it was a bathroom. He was proud that he did a lot of his best fucking in the bathroom. I'd lost count of the times that he'd had taken me in a stall at the arena.

"What the hell, Bryan? Why are you calling?"

I didn't hang around rethinking my question. "What am I to you? Partner, lover, boyfriend?"

Aarni let out a bark of a laugh, and it was hateful and dark. "You're a good fuck, kid. You know that is what you are to me."

"But—?"

"What the hell do you want me to say? I'm at a party for god's sake." Aarni sounded pissed.

I hung up. Guilt gripped me, along with anger and self-recrimination.

THE SEASON STARTED WITH A BANG, with me in my backup role riding the pine. Four games and the Railers took three of them as victories. I hadn't heard from Aarni since that night nor from Gatlin. That was okay though. I'd come to terms with messing things up with Gatlin. Aarni, on the other hand, was a raw despair I carried with me and examined at moments when my brain wasn't filled with hockey. It didn't help that we were starting our season with a West Coast stand, with the Raptors our first stop. Given that the two teams were in different conferences, the Railers only met the Raptors twice this season, once now, the other before Christmas. I dreaded the two games as equally as I needed to face them. Maybe Aarni would want me tonight if the Raptors won on their home ice?

Because today was the day that the Raptors met the Railers.

I wanted a chance to talk to Aarni, face-to-face, to apologize or shout or who the hell knew what. I missed Aarni so much. I missed the team.

And I feared what my place was on the Railers.

Was Aarni right when he'd warned me in the summer?

Was I only there as a placeholder until they found a real backup? Was Ten a bad person, a spoiled, temperamental celebrity who got his own way? Were the Railers a team who'd somehow cheated their way to winning the Stanley Cup? Or was it Aarni who was wrong?

Confusion and self-doubt were my friends in the dark nights, and I hated them with a passion.

Somehow, I managed to keep my head in the game during practice on the Raptors' ice. Standing here, looking up at the familiar rafters, walking past the home locker room to get to ours, I was quiet, but no one called me on it. Not even Ten who had taken to hovering around the net at practice today, half-working on tip-ins and half staring at me.

The Raptors were here, in this building. They'd had an hour out on the ice this morning, but there'd been no text from Aarni, nothing to even say hello. No one had reached out to me.

Coach called Stan and me in for a pregame meeting, Coach Gagnon there as well. The goalie coach was all kinds of serious.

"Bryan, I'm putting you in net," Coach Benning said and sat back in his chair expectantly.

What did he want me to do? Let out a yelp of excitement at getting my first Railers start on Raptor ice? Tears that I wasn't ready? Fear of facing my old team? I felt nothing. No fear or enthusiasm or sorrow.

"I'm excited about the opportunity," I murmured, the perfect soundbite that I'd give the waiting journalists when they asked me later.

After I fucked up and lost the game for the Railers.

"You know team," Stan said enthusiastically and clapped my shoulder.

"I do." I forced eagerness into my voice.

"Watch video," Stan announced, and Coach Gagnon opened the laptop. We sat for a while, watching highlights of the shooting from the Raptors in their first few season games. They'd lost two for two so far, and I knew what that meant. They would be messy and frantic for a win.

I wanted to warn Stan about some of the shit they pulled; how much they hated the Railers. Or at least, how much Aarni hated them. I did mention it to Connor, and the captain listened to my concerns, and I caught him glancing at Ten.

Ten was always the target for other teams, the one that they wanted to take out to level the playing field. But the Railers didn't only have Ten. We were a team, and I was backstopping that team in less than two hours.

Restless, I left the visitors' dressing rooms and turned left, away from the main entrance to the ice and up the stairs to the roof. This had always been my favorite place at the Raptors' arena, with views over Tucson and beyond. I snapped a couple of photos on my phone, something to remember this place by. I could show Gatlin,

Just as a friend.

"Thought I'd find you here."

I spun on my heels. Aarni was by the door, leaning on the jamb, smirking. I immediately had an image of Gatlin front and center, and I shook my head to clear it. Gatlin was slimmer, not so bulked up, his skin marked with colors, his expression happy. This man was Aarni, taller and bigger than me, and he wasn't happy. If anything, he looked pissed, and for a moment I felt as if I deserved his irritation. I needed to get off the roof and back down to the dressing room, suit up, and get in the zone, so I walked to the door, expecting Aarni to move to one side.

He didn't. He gripped my arm and held me still. "Meet

me after the game," he said, not leaving any room for me to disagree. "It'll be good to catch up."

"You mean fuck," I said softly and winced when his hold tightened. I attempted to slip away, but I wasn't ready to push him too far. He pressed me to the wall and pinned me there, with a hand on my chest and the other one twisted in my hair. He tugged to expose my throat, and I waited. He wasn't going to kiss me. He just liked it when I couldn't move.

"We could fuck now," Aarni suggested.

I shoved at him, testing his hold, but he slid his arm up, so it rested on my throat. The last time he'd fucked me, he'd held me there, so hard I'd seen spots in my vision, unable to think. The remembered fear took my breath, and I stiffened in his hold.

"Let me go," I said. Pleaded.

"You remember who looked after you," he growled and yanked my hair a little more, biting at my throat.

I needed to get away, wanted to tell him that I didn't need looking after, that no one needed to look after me at the Railers. But he wasn't listening, even as I attempted to string the sentences together. He spun me, and my face scraped the wall. He still had hold of my throat, and he pressed his erection against my ass.

"What the hell?" someone shouted, and with coursing fear, I recognized Ten's voice. "Let him go."

Aarni chuckled darkly. "If it isn't the boy wonder," he said to Ten. "You need to move on."

I moved the best I could against the brick, met Ten's gaze, and watched his concern morph into anger.

"We're going," he snapped.

"Fuck you," Aarni responded with heat.

Ten pushed a hand between us and then somehow was in the space, separating Aarni and me.

"We're going," he repeated, soft but firm.

I wriggled out from the Ten/Aarni weight and gripped Ten's arm. I had images of Aarni hitting Ten or pushing him down the stairs. "Come on Ten," I pleaded as Ten and Aarni faced off against each other.

I heard Aarni's dark chuckle. "See you on the ice, boys."

I led Ten down the steps, and wordlessly, he followed me until we were at the locker room door. Then he stopped me with a gentle hand on my arm.

"You want to report this? I can get Jared."

I huffed a laugh. Ten didn't understand a thing. That up there was my fault, and I'd very nearly gotten Ten involved in a situation he should be anywhere near. Then a thought hit me.

"What were you doing on the roof?"

"I followed you, wanted to talk to you, saw Aarni go up there, thought about how you've been, and decided to investigate," he explained as if it was every day that a teammate checked on my welfare.

"How I've been? What do you mean?"

"Quiet, thoughtful, not yourself since you left with Gatlin after the party. Did Gatlin do something to upset you? Should I talk to Stan about it? Or is this an Aarni thing? Is he your boyfriend?"

So many questions, and my head spun as I met Ten's earnest expression.

"It's nothing you need to worry about. I'm good." I pushed open the door. I had to get ready, focus, and Ten was up in my space, getting wrapped up in the mess. I didn't need that.

. . .

OUT ON THE ice for warmups, I stayed well and truly in my net and refused to check out the Raptors on their side of the ice. Teams had half the ice to skate on and test shots, and Stan and I took it in turns to stand in net. Ten skated over to me, stick-tapped my leg, and smiled at me. I grinned back at him and hoped to hell I faked it enough to reassure him. Up on that roof, I'd been frozen in indecision, and then Ten was there, warning Aarni away.

Wanting to know what was going on.

We headed back to the locker room, and I went into my bag, sent a quick text to Gatlin. A simple message that needed saying.

I want to see you. Kiss you. I need to talk.

Then, with confusion and pride and fear and hope all pushing for the room in my head, I skated out for the game and took up my position on the ice. The crowd booed as our team came out, wanting their displeasure to be heard, the loudest for Ten, who I'm sure was getting used to this by now. There was a video compilation of my pitiful showings for the Raptors, but the booing was all I could hear, and I wanted it over and done with.

The first shot on goal got past me, Aarni skating close after and smirking at me, winking.

Ten and Adler both came over to the net, nodded to me, reassured me. I looked over at the bench and to Stan.

Maybe it should be Stan out here. I'm going to choke again. The Raptors won the next face-off at center ice, and it was on, Ten taking the possession, a crisp pass to Lee, who sent it off the boards and onto Ten's waiting stick. All that tap-in practice paid off, the puck heading direct center, their goalie caught off to one side, and it was saved, but it was precisely what the Railers needed. A shot on goal at least and only one minute played.

They put Aarni out every shift against Ten, but Arvy protected him, worrying away at Aarni until it wasn't just me who could see the moment that Aarni let anger get the better of him. He tripped Arvy and was sent off for a two-minute penalty, which left the Railers on the power play with only a few seconds left in the first period.

Dieter ran with the opportunity, found the back of the opposition's net on his first power play shift, and like that we'd equaled the game.

The second period was frantic, and not one shot got past the Raptors' goalie or me. We were brick walls, and I don't know what it was about tonight, but the ice spoke to me, and I knew every move they were going to make. They were all over me in the net, Aarni deliberately barreling into me at least twice, neither of which he was called for. The cursing was loud enough for me to hear, the words designed to hurt.

I ignored it all.

It was Ten's game in the third period, his line scoring twice, taking it to three-one, and even though they tried hard to remove each member of our first line, somehow Ten, Troy and Lee made it out alive. The expression on Aarni's face was evident. He was furious. Slamming his stick and snapping it in two pieces on the bench was what I expected. When he caught me watching, he gestured to his eyes.

I'm watching you.

A three-one win, on the road, against the Raptors, and the flight back was jubilant, which carried me along. We were going back home, and I had only one thing on my mind. I didn't overanalyze my feelings, didn't give any thought to the anxiety that still churned inside me, but when I finally pulled out my cell, I saw I had a message from Gatlin.

I miss you. And then, more importantly, he said what I wanted to hear. *I want to kiss you again.*

I was *so* up for that.

TEN

Gatlin

I had a checklist. Me. A checklist. If Garrett knew this, the shit talk would never end. But I wanted to make sure everything was right. Things were checked on the list. *Everything* was checked on the list.

Food. Homemade spaghetti with meatballs and a tossed salad. Check.

Wine. A cheeky little zinfandel. Check.

Music. Priest, AC/DC, Sabbath, and some Emerson, Lake & Palmer if things took a passionate turn. Check.

Atmosphere. Lights low and candles on the kitchen table. Check.

Showered, neatly trimmed and dapper host nicely decked out in black jeans, a white shirt, and black leather vest as well. Check.

Condoms. Just in case. Check.

Lube. Also, just in case. Check.

NOW WE NEEDED the other half of the equation. I checked my phone for the eight hundredth time in an hour.

Why I was so edgy was a mystery. I had the night well in hand and had planned for any contingency that might come up. Wow, that was laced with innuendo. Or was it only my dirty mind?

A sharp rap on the door yanked me out of my fog. I ran my hands over my hair, blew out a breath, and went to open it. Bryan stood on my tiny little porch, his smile tentative. The black stray cat rubbed around his legs.

"He's looking for dinner. Come in." I waved him in. He looked so damn good, so tall and so wide across the shoulders. "Just let me feed him, and then I'll toss the pasta into the pot. Take off your coat."

"Is he coming inside then?" I heard him ask as I grabbed the bag of tuna and egg-flavored dry cat food.

"Nah, he's still not mine, but we talked one night and bonded. Or something." I gave Bryan a weak smile and went outside to dump some food into the cat's little dish. It was a cute thing with fish and tiny paw prints on it. I'd seen it at the grocery store when I went to pick up our dinner fixings. The stray purred loudly and dove into his dinner. I ran a hand down his back, once, because anything more made him edgy and he ran away. Not unlike the striking man waiting inside for me.

"There. All fed. He'll curl up in that old box with the blanket after he eats."

"Have you given him a name?"

"No, he's not mine."

"I love this album," Bryan changed the subject, referring to *Master of Reality* thumping out of the speakers. "I think Ozzy is one of my top five favorite singers."

"Oh yeah, Oz is a beast."

He followed me into the kitchen.

I tossed the cat food back into the cupboard and washed my hands. "You can get the wine out and pour it if you're in the mood for it. If not, there's beer and soda in there."

"Wine is fine." He busied himself with uncorking the bottle and pouring us both a decent amount in the wine glasses I'd borrowed from Jess. Our fingers brushed when he handed me my glass. "I'm feeling awkward tonight."

"Maybe this will help." I stole a soft kiss.

His lips pulled up into a small smile that made the candlelight glow a bit brighter.

"Can we talk before we put the pasta in?"

"Sure." I motioned toward my living room with my wine glass. We settled onto the couch, and I turned the volume down on Oz a few notches.

"Right, so, there's a lot of things that I want to say to you." *Children of the Grave* began playing as he fidgeted with his glass, his gaze on the wine inside that glass.

"Take your time." I ran my free hand down his arm and took a sip of the cheeky zinfandel. It was quite good. "We have all night."

His lips twisted into a kind of smile. "My boyfriend, his name was Aarni."

Ah okay. I caught that *was* right off, so yay for past tense. And Aarni? Did he mean Aarni from the Raptors? A hockey player? I didn't ask him to confirm that, just listened to him talk.

"He was a toxic, controlling jerk who meant nothing. I thought he did…or I guess I thought I meant something to him… but I didn't. He just got off on abusing me and hurting me."

"I'm sorry. I know how much losing someone you care about hurts." Oh boy, did I. I had a hole the size of the Railers' Zamboni smack dab in the middle of my heart.

"Well, he's not worth my pain, but it…. yeah…it

hurts." His dark eyes lifted from his wine, and I kind of fumbled around in them for a minute or two.

How had a man of my experience fallen so damn hard so damn fast?

"That part of my life is done. Arizona and Aarni are in my past. This town and this team are what's important to me now. I want to stay with the Railers. They're a great team. I mean, they care, truly *care* about each other. I want to fight for my place on the team. I need to build a good thing for myself, and that's not just for work. Mitch said I have to find what makes me happy and fulfilled and fight for the things that do. You and the Railers make me feel good, as if I can be a whole man again."

I sat there like a drunken frog on a log, staring, my ears hearing the words but my brain unable to get them lined up so that they made sense. I wasn't sure who this Mitch was, but he seemed to be talking some good talk to Bryan.

"Are you saying that you want to try to make a thing here with me?"

He nodded and bit down on his lower lip. "If you want to try to make a thing with me, yeah. I mean, I totally get that you'd be sick of my shit. How I keep bolting when we get close. If you don't want me, then I—"

"Bryan, maybe we should put our wine down." His expressive brows dropped in confusion. "I'd really like to take you into my bedroom and show you just how much I want you, but I'd hate to spill the wine. It's too tasty to end up on the floor."

A slow, brilliant smile was his reply. He put his wine glass on the coffee table. I did the same. Then I stood and offered him my hand. When he stood, he slid his fingers between mine. He ducked his head down to taste my mouth. I lapped at his lips, eager to spread the taste of that tart zinfandel all over his tongue.

Our progress to the bedroom was slow. We had to stop and kiss, touch, peel off clothing, and locate ELP's master-piece, *Brain Salad Surgery*, before we could fall into my freshly made bed. Which was another thing on the list. Make that two things.

CLEAN SHEETS. Check.

One of the hottest men ever to grace my life lying naked on those clean sheets. Big check.

WHEN I SAY HOT, I mean a masculine, incendiary beauty that made me slack-witted. He was the athletic form. Like a sculpture of an ancient Grecian gladiator, his body was long and firm, muscled and ripped, hair the color of mahogany ran from his chest to his cock, surrounding it with a bush of curls. His balls hung between his legs, fine dark hair covering them, begging me to cup and cradle them. The man was a sensual masterpiece who had somehow ended up in my bed. I should pay homage to his perfection.

I slithered up over Bryan, eager to get to it, yet sensing he needed a slow hand. Toxic and abusive. That was what he'd said his last lover had been. Then he would need tender touches, soft thrusts and lots of endearments. Those I could supply. Kissing him started timidly. He was hard, yes. Apparently, his body was there and into things, but I wanted all of him there, not just a stiff prick.

Taking my time, I tasted him and eased him as best I could. Tasting his mouth and elbows, his knees and, yes, those beautiful balls of his, and then taking his cock into my mouth. It was heavenly, his taste, salty pre-cum resting on my tongue before I sucked him deep into my throat. He gyrated under me, hips punching upward. I wanted more. Needed to taste every inch of him this night because God knew I would somehow fuck this up, and he would be gone. Like Rex, like Gina, probably like that damn cat sleeping outside my back door.

"Mm, yeah," he moaned as I licked a wet trail from his cock to his chest, flicking his nipple until he arched up into me, his hands wound in the crisp, clean sheets. I took him in hand and stroked. The man was well-hung, long and thick. When he arched, he *really* arched. His heels dug into the mattress, and his back bowed a foot off the bed. Flexibility, thy name is Bryan Delaney.

I slipped off him, laughing. He covered me then, those powerful skater's legs tangling with mine, his mouth hot and greedy. I let him lead. His teeth scored my throat. His tongue followed a line of ink across my shoulder and down my arm. Cocks bumped, fingers clutched, and groans filled the room.

"Fuck me." I panted as I grabbed his ass. Firm muscle filled my palms. I squeezed hard, getting a grunt from the man gyrating away on top of me.

His head came up from my neck, where he'd been sucking a mark that I'd probably carry for two weeks. Not that I minded a love mark from my glorious young lover, but I suspected my employees and brother would have comments.

"What? No. You don't really…" I saw the confusion in his dark eyes. His cock rested beside mine, both flattened between us. "I never did that for….you sure?"

"I am *positive*. I'm versatile. Fuck me, Bryan, and then next time, if you want, I'll get inside of you."

He lowered his head to capture my mouth, his body throwing off some incredible heat. I wrapped myself around his long, strong form, eager to feel him moving inside me. When the kiss broke, we worked on getting him ready. Condom and lube, both of us fumbling and chuckling at our ineptitude.

"Watch me," I said. He positioned my foot on his shoulder, his gaze jumping from my face to my ass as I worked two fingers into myself. "Shit." Oh hell, that was nice. And hot. Him kneeling between my thighs, his cock just a few inches from my hole...

"Shit, that's...yeah, you need to get in me." That sounded bossy. "Sorry, no, do what you want." I slid my fingers out of my ass, and he moved to replace them instantly, the fat head of his cock slipping inside. I said words. I mean, I *think* they were words. Inch by inch, he filled me, his brown gaze moving over us, from where we were joined, to my face, then over my chest and back to his dick deep inside of me.

"I want to love you," he whispered, his long fingers wrapped around my ankle. "I've never been allowed to love another man like this."

"Then love me, Bryan."

He fell over me, catching his weight on his hands, and moved his hips. He watched, intently, as I writhed and whimpered in pleasure. I wondered if he was lost in that vision of his. I grabbed the back of his neck with both hands, rolled my hips, and held on tight.

"Do not hold back," I huffed.

He didn't.

Bryan fucked into me so hard I yelped, and he paused, worry deep on his face.

"No! Oh, shit, no, do *not* stop. Love me, Bryan." I clenched around him, and his eyes rolled back. Then, he gave himself over to the pleasure of my body gripping his. He moved with grace and power, slamming into me over and over, his grunts and hisses spurring me along until I shot all over my chest. Bryan went deep twice more and then blew apart. I tried to hold onto him, but our skin was too sweaty to get a good grip. When the tremors rumbling through him subsided, he fell on me. I kissed his face, getting my lips to his cheek before he shimmied off me, mumbling something that got buried in the rumpled bedding.

"Holy fuck knuckles," I gasped, my breathing far from normal. I let my eyes drift shut as he lay beside me, tacky skin clinging to tacky skin.

Bryan managed to roll to his side, his hand coming to my chest. He rubbed at a few droplets of semen with a finger. I opened my eyes and turned my head in his direction.

"I love loving you," he whispered, grabbing a sultry kiss before he had to leave the bed to attend to the condom. While he was down the hall in the bathroom, I sat up gingerly, feeling a slight twinge here and there. I stared down at my toes, letting my body cool a bit while giving the man some privacy. I heard the gentle slap of bare feet come into the bedroom, the floorboard by the door creaking. Then the bed sagged. He sat behind me and passed a damp cloth around to me. Thanking him, I wiped myself clean, then threw the washcloth at the hamper in the corner.

"This on your back... this ink. It's amazing." His fingers danced up my spine, making me shudder. "This angel is stunning. What does this mean?"

This was not supposed to be the topic of discussion. We were supposed to talk about, romantic things now. Not this. He traced a long white wing with one rough fingertip. Starting from the middle of my back out over my right shoulder, his touch went, making it harder and harder for me to sit there quietly.

"It's my sister," I said, praying Emerson, Lake & Palmer would drown my words. He sat up, his palm resting on my lower back, right where the gossamer edges of Gina's robes would be. "She died when she was ten."

"I'm so sorry." He moved around me and leaned into my side, his shoulder behind mine, and pressed a kiss to my throat. "Was she sick?"

"No." I wasn't sure I should go on. I mean, who was this man, really? We'd fucked once. That gave him no right to see my sickly innards.

"If you don't want to talk about it…"

I lifted my chin and turned to find his beautifully sad gaze on me. "If I tell you, will you promise not to leave me tonight? I won't ask more of you than that, just this one night."

I wished he would have spoken, but he gave me a bob of his head, so I took that as his vow that he would stay the night. It was all I could ask of him.

"My parents had gone to Virginia for a weekend when Gina was ten. They left her home with me. Garrett had long since moved out, and I was in my senior year, getting ready to graduate and join the Navy."

"Is that why you have Polynesian stuff on your arm and all that sea stuff here?" He patted my chest.

"Yeah, got my first tat when I was eighteen from a shop two blocks from the base. I was hooked. They're kind of addictive." Sitting there with him, in my home, in my bed, listening to one of the greatest bands ever, made me feel as if I could maybe tell this story without losing my shit. "Vowed I would learn the trade as soon as I was discharged, which I did."

He never prodded when I fell into silence or paused to gather my strength.

"Right. So Gina. I was watching her. It was the

weekend and early. She woke me up to have breakfast with her. We had cereal. Cocoa Rice. It made the milk all chocolatey, and she loved that." I smiled at the memory of that last smile of Gina's. "She wanted to go outside and play with her friends, but none of them were up yet. I told her to play in the backyard while I took care of the dishes. She went outside, calling to me that I had better not be too long or she'd turn the hose on me. She liked to do that. Surprise you with a hose blast." I smiled over the flare of pain.

And this was where it got bad. The crushing weight of it all began pressing down on me, making breathing and talking hard. Bryan rubbed that angel on my back, the one with the bright blue eyes and flowing hair. The one that was my baby sister as I wanted to remember her.

"I loaded the dishwasher and started a load of washing. Mom hated coming home to piles of dirty laundry or dishes. Then I made a fast pass through the living room to tidy up where we'd watched movies the previous night. All totaled maybe fifteen minutes…"

Bryan said nothing, just moved his hand in a tight circle. I sucked it up and forged on. In for a miserable penny as they say…

"When I— When I stepped out into the backyard, I saw her lying on the grass. Nothing new, right, because she would do that on occasion. Lie on her belly to study a caterpillar or a dandelion or stretch out on her back to study clouds. Gina was a dreamer." Another pause to gather my strength. "It was when I walked up to her and asked her what she was looking at this time that I saw something was wrong. She uh…she wasn't moving or breathing. I knelt beside her and saw that she had vomit on her lips and chin."

And yet another pause, this time to push back at the

memories. They rushed over me anyway, every damn second of that morning, like a tsunami.

"I had no idea what to do. I tried to do CPR, but it was too late. She'd been dead for too long when I finally got to her. They said she had a seizure. What they used to call a grand mal, but they now call them SUDEP. Sudden unexpected death in epilepsy. It was the first seizure she had ever had, and when she went down, she fell on her back and choked to death on her own vomit."

I wiped at my mouth with the back of my hand unconsciously, to clear away the memory of that day when I'd put my lips to Gina's and tried to blow life back into her.

The shaky breath I sucked in failed to stem the short, violent sob that got out. They always did, those fucking sobs. They broke free whenever I talked about Gina's death. Which is why I didn't talk about it much.

Bryan slid his arm around me and held me close.

"My family kind of fell apart after I let that happen. The Navy was the only thing that kept me from drinking myself to death. My parents won't talk to me, and my brother really kind of hates me. Shit. Sorry, this is hard. It was my fault that she died. If I would have just gone out with her when she....when she asked the first time."

I coughed and sputtered, dragged my hand over my face. The heaves set in. Then the shakes. And then, the silent tears. And through it all Bryan sat beside me, embracing me, whispering that it was not my fault, that sometimes good people die young, and that I was not to blame for God's plans.

When the worst of the ugly was over, I was curled into his side, my cheek on his chest, his fingers back to tracing Gina's wings.

"So, wow, we're having us some fun times tonight," I choked out, hoping to get us out of this shitty pit of despair we were in. "Want to play some Uno or something?"

"We could eat but maybe later. Right now, though, let's just hold each other. I need it."

"Yeah, so do I." I cupped his beautiful face in my hands and kissed him with everything that was left inside of me, which probably wasn't much, but what there was I gave to him. "Thank you for not sprinting for the door."

He pulled me closer, his arm over my back, and we lay back down and pulled the covers up over us.

"You listened to my bad stuff and didn't throw me out," he said, his voice soft and low, his fingers moving through my hair. My cheek was on the beefy part of his arm. His chest rose and fell sharply. "You have no idea the things that I allowed him to do to me. The things that I helped him do to other people. I hurt people too, Gat."

I rolled into him a bit, enough to press a kiss to his chest.

Maybe, just maybe, the two of us could help the other learn how to move past the horrible mistakes that plagued us? Could the healing start tonight, with this embrace?

ELEVEN

Bryan

"Where did you get this scar?"

Gatlin had woken me up with coffee and pressing kisses to the top of my spine. Gentle kisses and whispered words of good morning, and I'd been lulled into the peace of it all. I'd drunk my coffee, relaxed too much, and he'd found the scar.

It curved from behind my hip bone and ended close to my spine, a pale pucker of flesh that was a reminder of a fight I wished I could forget, particularly with everything that had happened since. It wasn't obvious in the half dark, but in daylight, it was plain to see.

I rolled onto my back quickly, and pulled Gatlin close, distracting him from his question, knowing I wasn't ready to explain.

"Kiss me," I ordered him.

He pulled back a little and smiled down at me.

"Stop changing the subject."

"I wasn't," I denied and kissed him again. This time the desperation to stop him talking was real. We'd done enough talking last night, and I didn't think it was all we'd be doing.

What about sex? Why weren't we having more sex?

I slid my hands down his back, imagining the angel, tracing his muscles, until I could grip his ass and grind up against him. That stopped him wanting to talk. He groaned into the kiss, and then somehow, he got free from my hold, sitting up and on his knees and staring down at me. He was hard. This wasn't about not being turned on. So why was he stopping?

"Bryan, where did the scar come from?"

"Why is it important?"

"It wasn't," Gatlin began with measured patience, "but you didn't want to talk about it, so I figure it means something to you."

"It's nothing."

"Was it a skating incident?"

Gatlin waited for me to answer, and at that moment, I could've said yes, and it would've been gone and done with, he would've believed me and moved on. His beautiful eyes were filled with so much compassion, and after what he'd shared with me last night, was this one thing I could share with him?

"Kind of," I hedged and then sighed noisily when the lie tasted bitter on my tongue. "No." I didn't know what else to say. I had imagined telling *someone* someday about what happened, but in my head, it had been Aarni who listened to me and understood my story. Aarni who was my knight in shining armor.

"Wait there," Gatlin instructed and padded, gloriously nude, over to a cabinet in the corner of the room. I hadn't really looked at it before, but notebooks were strewn on it, along with a pot of pencils. He chose the top book, and I recognized his sketchpad, which he brought back to the bed. Taking up his position sitting cross-legged opposite me, he then opened the pad and placed it in front of me.

"Look," he said, and I was relieved he'd stopped the line of questioning.

I examined the drawing, my chest tight at the art. It was stunning, the sweeps of blue and the edgy touch of a steampunk owl against the steam of an old-style locomotive, iron engine. He'd sketched a couple more views of the same design. In the center was a compass, with the compass points fading into the blur.

"What does the compass mean?"

"I feel like hockey is your home, and that your life expands away from it."

I listened to what he said and felt unaccountably sad at the words. I did have a family. Daisy, George, Emma, and Tom might have been a temporary billet family, but I had grown up with them in the three years I'd lived in Erie. I needed to tell Gatlin that, but I didn't have the words in my head.

"That's perfect," I murmured.

"Hey, you know who Matt Groening is?" he asked.

I looked up at him. "He's the dude who draws the *Simpsons*."

"Yeah, and did you know that when he originally drew Homer, he deliberately put his initials into the shapes of Homer's hairline and ear? I mean, he changed his mind about the G in the ear, but the M of Homer's hair is still there."

I wasn't sure where this was going, but it almost sounded like Gatlin was leading up to something. Knowing Gatlin, it would be artistically profound; I loved that passion in him.

"I didn't know that."

He dipped his gaze momentarily as if he were embarrassed, then pointed to one of the detailed feathers vanishing into a stylized clock piece. "I do a similar thing in my helmet designs." He traced what I could see was actually a G.

"Wow, so there's a G on Stan's as well?"

"Look at the Noah-bunny, and you'll see it in the curve of the furry ears."

"I will. Actually, I had a thought that maybe we should wait on my helmet."

"You don't have to say you like the design if you don't," Gatlin murmured.

I looked at him, horrified that he even thought I would do that. He was different. I felt like I could be totally honest with him, and how the hell had that happened? I'd only known him a short while, but somehow, he was the first person I'd ever wanted to confide in outside of Daisy.

Don't trust him. He'll just end up laughing at you.

I pushed the little voice in my head that sounded so much like Aarni, to one side.

"I love it. I just don't want you to get this done only for me to get moved down to the minors or traded to another team."

I shrugged as I said it as if it didn't matter to me whether or not I stayed.

He laced his fingers with mine. "They'd be idiots to let you go. You're exactly what the Railers' need, someone effective as a backup to Stan, one day to be the starting goalie."

"From your mouth…" I muttered.

"Have they said something to you?"

I blinked at him, analyzing the things that I had been told. There were key words that kept appearing in pep talks from the coaches. Promise. Stability. Trust. Along with the long-term plan for my role that Alain Gagnon had handed me where I was training with Stan, supporting him, working hard for the team.

The team that appeared to like me. Hope poked at my heart, and at the same moment, I realized I was staring at Gatlin.

"No, they want to work with me; they traded for me. I have to believe that I will be there a while if I work hard."

"I'll start the helmet design soon then?"

This was a question, not a statement, and I didn't have to weigh up the options for an answer. Even if I did get traded to the opposite end of the country, I would at least have some of Gatlin's art to take with me and a reminder of the Railers who seemed nothing but kind to me.

"Yeah. I guess so."

"How did you get the scar, Bryan?" he asked, so softly I almost missed it. Peace evaporated from my mind, and I was thrust back to the last few days at my childhood home.

"I got into a fight. Not a hockey fight." I stopped and considered the best way to approach this. I didn't want or need pity, so a clinical recital was best. I took a deep breath and spoke. "I had this good friend, Darren. We were super close, ended up falling into kissing. His uncle, a pastor, caught us and lectured us on evil, and my friend toed the line, ended up getting married. I wasn't going to change myself because of religion. Only my mom was devastated at my mortal sin, and my dad, who liked his drink, decided to use his fists on me. I was fifteen, and I fought back. I fell through the patio window and was cut. I was lucky it didn't sever an artery or anything. It's an ugly scar, but that was a violent time."

It was a relief to get everything out, but I burned with shame and was scared that he would look at me differently.

Silence. I waited for Gatlin to say something, anything,

or smile or frown, but all I could see was that he swallowed, and his eyes were bright with emotion.

"Okay," he began and squeezed my hand. "Then how about we take that scar you think is ugly and make it into something beautiful?"

One-handed, he sketched my owl and the compass and threw in the hint of a puck in 3D denting my skin. It shouldn't have worked, but it did.

"Just black and gray for most of it, or maybe shades of brown and copper, but a hint of color in the bird's eyes."

I watched him draw, marveling at the magic he created, but I didn't understand at first. Then he pushed the pad toward me and turned it around.

"Tattoos to cover scars can look really good. The skin is sensitive, but you can make it work. Then there wouldn't be a scar. There would be the midnight hunter, with your crazy vision, and the anchor of hockey in the compass and the puck."

I looked from the drawing to his face and back again.

"You amaze me," I whispered.

"I could do something else. It's up to you." He wrinkled his nose as he spoke, all kinds of modest.

"No! I want this."

He chuckled and leaned in for a kiss.

"How about you tell me when you're ready for me to start. I could take it slowly, do it when the shop isn't open, make it *really* personal." He waggled his eyebrows, teasing me with the thought of how much fun *really personal* could be.

Abruptly, I wanted him under me or over me or in me. As long as we were doing something that involved a lot of close and personal contact, I didn't care.

I loved the designs. The fact that the compassion he showed to me wasn't pitying. As he kissed me deeply, all I could think was that it would be effortless to fall in love with Gatlin.

If I let myself.

AARNI HADN'T CALLED for so long I'd almost forgotten he'd ever been part of my life. I received what sounded like a pocket dial from a bar. There was no message but receiving that meant my name must have been on a list to be dialed in the first place. He had to have my number still.

How did that make me feel? Confused as to why he hadn't phoned to apologize for what happened. Or maybe puzzled about why he hadn't called to lecture me.

Not one part of it made me feel as if I'd drawn a line under Aarni, but at practice, I'd worked so hard as I considered the issue that Stan took a seat and decided to watch me as the team fired pucks on net. Of course, he didn't sit for long, but it was enough for the whole team to comment on me sucking up to the coaches.

Said with affection.

Adler seemed intent on working up his best chirps. The amount of time he spent getting up in my personal space was comical, and he gave up trying to rile me as Ten took a shot, then spent a long time attempting to get a goal past my blocker. It wasn't happening, and in the end, it was me chirping him.

"I thought you were good at this?" I said as he skated backward.

He gave me the finger, but he was grinning ear to ear. Like he loved shooting on *me*, as if he maybe liked *me*.

Practice done, and with no thoughts of Aarni in my head, the buzz of hockey and life flowing through my veins, I made my way to my stall. In the practice facility, I was on the end, but that didn't make me feel isolated. If anything, it gave me a little space from the teasing and laughing and pranks, so I could get into my headspace if I needed to. Although no one had pranked me yet, but that was okay. I know that no one fucked with Stan because he was unpredictably Russian and likely to sit on the perpetrator. So maybe goalies were off-limits?

I never even thought about why there was only one bottle of shampoo on the side, when there was usually a selection that was permanently on offer to the players, or why I was the only guy in the showers or hell, why any of this mattered. I just knew that it was hot water, and I closed my eyes and tilted my head forward so the water could ease the tension in my shoulders. The shampoo smelled of rose or something else weird. I dried myself off and crossed to the mirrors.

I was blue. In streaks down my face and body.

I grinned at my reflection.

Damn it, I was Railers' blue. I was a goalie smurf, and I loved it.

No one claimed responsibility, but Adler whistled way more than average, and I saw him high-fiving Lester and Connor.

This was so on.

When I arrived at the tattoo shop, my overnight bag in hand, Gatlin stared at the blue streaks with wide eyes as I explained that this would *only last a day or so.* He snorted a laugh and kissed me. Then, when the shop was shut, he proceeded to kiss all the blue parts he could find. He apparently had a kink for color, and I resolved right there to be the most colorful person I could be. For him.

If we played at home, I stayed over at the shop. When we were away, Gatlin and I FaceTimed. I had to have my daily fix of him, and he made me smile so wide that sometimes, one of the team would poke me and ask me what the joke was.

Stan kind of summed it all up. "You smile big as biggest big thing." Or at least I think he meant that because some of it was in Russian.

Coming into November, I felt like one of the team, someone whose opinion mattered, and the Railers were holding their position at third in the conference. I'd had seven starts so far, won four, lost two, and taken one game to overtime, which Ten had won for us with one of the best goals of the season so far.

We rocked this hockey thing, and I was happy in the small apartment over the tattoo shop, and the tattoo on my hip was starting to take shape. Gatlin was focused when he worked on my skin. I stared at him, teased him, tried to make him laugh. It was as if the real me was coming out from his shell, the one who'd deliberately held back after what had happened at fifteen with my birth parents.

Tonight, Daisy and George were in the arena to watch us play Columbus, fighting for the points to get us to second on the table. Gatlin was at a training event and wouldn't be back until later, but he would get to meet them. I wasn't in goal.

That was planned for the weekend matchup against one of our Pennsylvania rivals, which they were staying for. That meant I had time to focus on *them*. After the game, I brought both in to meet everyone on the team. Daisy had that thing for Ten, and Ten was happy to get a long hug and promised to give her a signed puck.

"How about a jersey as well?" Ten asked and reached into his bag to pull out a spare. Damned wonder boy had spare jerseys on him at all times, *for his fans*. I'd noticed some Delaney jerseys in the crowds that attended the games, and I made a note to have a few spare to give out when I met anyone who knew me.

"She's my mom, and she'll want one of mine," I interjected, pouting at Ten and pasting a suitably hurt expression on my face. Daisy stopped in her gentle flirting with Ten and the team and rounded on me, her eyes wide.

"Bryan?"

"What?"

"You called me 'Mom,'" she said and pulled me in for a hug. I don't know why it was a shock; she'd been my real mom since I was fifteen. "You've never actually called me that."

Oh.

I didn't realize I'd held that back. We hugged, and she pulled me down to whisper in my ear.

"I'm still taking Ten's jersey," she teased. "But I do love you, sweetheart."

"Love you, Mom." Then I turned to George, who was discussing with Connor some move Gretzky had pulled in the seventies that Dad had witnessed. "I love you too," I said to him and poked him in the arm. "Dad."

He looked at me and then at Mom, puzzled, and then he hugged me. "Love you too, son."

Everything was perfect. Tonight, I might tell Gatlin how I was feeling.

When we all ended back at Stan and Erik's place, Mom and Dad were welcomed in, and I was so proud of them. When Gatlin arrived a little later, I introduced them as my mom and dad, which of course made my mom go all gooey and huggy.

Gatlin talked to Dad for the longest time, both seeming so serious, but I let it run its course.

"Your young man is lovely," Mom said, catching me coming from the kitchen with a plate of nachos. She stole a handful and then pressed a kiss to my cheek. "I can tell your dad likes him as well."

"I love him," I blurted and could have bitten my tongue. I didn't want my pronouncement of love to be heard by some random Railers member stealing their own supply of chips and dips from Stan's massive kitchen.

She just patted me on the chest. "I know you do."

Gatlin and I dropped them back to their hotel, and I was quiet in the car on the way back to his apartment, the darkness inviting all kinds of secrets.

"I love you," I said as dramatically as I had announced it to my mom. We were halfway home and just about to turn at a light.

Gatlin side-eyed me, took the turn, then indicated and pulled over at the next clear spot. He kissed me then, deep and never-ending, and it was a mark on me I would never want to erase.

"I love you too," he murmured against my lips and then continued the drive home.

Yeah. Life is good.

TWELVE

Gatlin

His back to my chest, the heavy breathing of a man close to the edge, filling my room and my soul, my hand tightly fisted around his cock. This was how every morning should start. Bryan pumped into my fingers, his skin flushed and sticky-damp with sweat that I lapped up greedily. My cock rested between his tight ass cheeks, spent, my spunk on his lower back after he had begged me to pull out, toss the condom, and come on him.

"Love you," I murmured into his shoulder. His cock kicked, covering my fingers and the sheets. Bryan gasped and fucked my hand, his firm hold gripping my wrist.

"Oh fuck." He panted as his body drew up tight, right down to his toes digging into the dirty sheets. "Love you… too."

I rained a storm of small kisses along his neck and ear, milking him until the tremors subsided and he melted into my arms.

"Better now?"

He nodded, his chest rising and falling at a somewhat reasonable pace.

The man had been beyond tense since November had edged its way toward December. Tomorrow was Thanksgiving, a meal that he and I would create and share here. A week after that, on December first, the Raptors arrived in Harrisburg. With each passing day, I felt his anxiety rise a little more and a little more.

Words were not really working to lessen his worry. The sex did the job quite well, and I was thrilled to rid him of that stress as often as he needed. Rutting like wild stags would only work for so long, and then he'd be back to the man I'd first met. Jumpy, scared, living in a state of perpetual anxiety. All because of Aarni, that motherfucking abusive cockmonkey. If I'd have had access to a city trash truck, I'd have driven to Arizona, found that sleazy, pig-faced bastard, and run him over. Then backed up and run him over again. I might have continued doing that until Aarni Lankinen was nothing more than a red grease spot on the street.

"Good. We have a lot of prep work to do for tomorrow. Your mother's stuffing recipe calls for oysters." I nuzzled the base of his neck, nipping a little as he turned to pudding in my arms. "I'll run to the store and grab some. I love your mother."

"Mm, yeah? Why? Because she shared her stuffing recipe with you?"

"Because she calls me a young man."

He laughed sleepily and drifted off, sated and secure and safe. And that was how he would stay. I would protect him with my life if need be. I held him for a long time, marveling at how fucking lucky I was to have this man. Then, sadly, the demand to pee grew too strong to ignore. I pressed a kiss to his back, right where all that new color and design now rested. Then I covered him up and started the day. Piss, shower, screw the shaving, since Bryan said he liked the silver whiskers.

After the coffee had brewed, I filled up a mug and went downstairs to find the newspaper and check for sales on oysters. If there was such a thing as a sale on oysters. Garrett was turning the key in the lock when I yanked the door open, startling him so badly he dropped his satchel.

"Dammit," he snarled over my sniggers. After he composed himself, I shut and locked the door behind him. I had two whole days off, and I did not want some walk-in sneaking in when I wasn't aware. Two days with Bryan. Talk about the perfect way to celebrate a holiday all about thanks. Well, Bryan and the guests we were having over for dinner. "You're chipper. Must be that young pup warming your bed?"

"Must be," I threw him a grin and a salacious wink.

A small smile pulled at his thin lips. "I'm happy for you then."

"Yeah?" I paused by the cash register where Jess usually crammed the mail.

"You sound surprised." He lifted my mug of coffee from my hand, took a sip, grimaced, and then handed it back.

"Well, I kind of am, to be honest. I thought you and the folks only wanted to see me suffer."

"Oh, for fuck sake, Gatlin!" Garrett shouted, slamming his leather bag filled with important banking type papers onto the glass counter. That brought my head up from the grocery store advertisement search. "I wish I knew where the hell you ever got the idea that I wanted you to suffer!"

"I let her die."

He gawked at me for several long seconds. I bent back down to poke around under the register. When I straightened, empty-handed, his expression had shifted from anger to one of mild aggravation. He sighed, fixed his tie that had blown free of his vest when he'd whacked the counter with his satchel, and pinned me down with a look.

"Gatlin, you did not *let* her die."

"But—"

He threw up a hand to slice off my words like a hatchet. "No, for once, just for one damn time, would you listen to me? I have never held you accountable for Gina's death. That seizure could have come on her at any time. Sadly, it hit when she was alone. No, do not speak, just listen to me just for once! You were a fine older brother; we both were. We adored her. We spoiled her. We doted on her. But no person can be with another person every minute of every day. You've carried this burden for twenty years, and it's an unneeded yoke."

I studied him intently, the mug of coffee resting in my shaky hand. "Mom and Dad hold me responsible."

"Which is why I've not spoken to them since the day of Gina's funeral."

Wow. That was news to me. I'd known they'd been estranged for some time but never really understood why. Garrett wasn't one to talk. Guess that was a brotherly trait.

"I just wish I knew how to talk to *you*." He added.

He stared at me, and I stared at him.

"Okay, well, thanks for not hating me. I thought you did."

His nose twitched a bit. A sign that he was still mildly upset.

"You would have known if you ever talked to me and not assumed the worst."

Right. Well, that kind of thing went two ways, but meh, I was tired and smitten and did not want to nitpick with him. I made a move to give an awkward hug over the counter, but he drew back slightly.

"No need to pretend that we're suddenly this incredibly demonstrative family," he mumbled under his breath, but he did offer me his hand. I took it, and we shook. Jess must've gotten her hug-it-out attitude from some potential emotional gene from a bygone ancestor because she sure as *hell* did not get it from either side of her parental tree.

Someone cleared their throat, and both Garrett and I glanced to the right. There stood Bryan, in soft fleece pants, ratty sneakers, a tank top that showed those magnificent shoulders and arms to the world, a wickedly dark love mark on his neck, and some incredible bedhead. So yes, the most beautiful man in the world was giving me a raised eyebrow.

"Oh, sorry. Bryan Delaney, this is my older brother, Garrett." I motioned to Garrett, who then walked to Bryan and offered him his hand. "Garrett, my boyfriend, Bryan."

Bryan threw me a shy smile. We'd not really used such a formal label before now. It felt right.

"Nice to meet you. Gatlin talks about you all the time. Are you coming for Thanksgiving dinner tomorrow? My parents are flying in for a couple of days."

My brother checked back with me, his hand still in my lover's. I nodded. Garrett gave me a soft inclination of his head.

"I'll be coming alone. My wife is in Nantucket with her grandparents. Oh. I should pass along the invitation to Jess." Garrett released Bryan's hand. I glanced up at the ceiling and rubbed at my chin whiskers and heard Garrett's long-suffering sigh. "She's been invited already, hasn't she?"

I started to say something. Bryan did as well. Garrett shook his head and chuckled. I gave him a shit-eating grin.

"Bring some of that expensive cold duck that you horde like Scrooge does halfpennies," I said.

Garrett rolled his eyes, and I knew then that things were okay between us. We might not be the sibling ideal, but at least I knew he cared, in his cold-fish sort of way. Some famous Greek, Prometheus maybe, said that big things have small beginnings. Perhaps my brother and I were destined for big things.

THE RAPTORS HAD FLOWN into town.

Since Stan had been in net the previous night against New Jersey, and because Bryan knew the team so well, my man was between the pipes. He'd fallen into this kind of eerie calm before leaving for the game. Unable to describe it any other way, I felt he had gotten into the place that goalies go before a game where it is mental preparation. Sitting in a lovely spacious seat called the "Steamers Section," I had some corporate types on either side of me, which was fine. Me in my Delaney jersey, tattered jeans, and beat-to-hell shitkickers didn't stand out at all among the expensive suits. Nope. Not at all. Garrett would have felt right at home.

As soon as the puck drop at center ice started the game, things got intense. Both teams had that edge, and every chance to finish a check was taken. Usually, this kind of aggressive play was reserved for those interstate rivalries or playoff games. Big men were slammed into the boards by other big men steadily. Small scuffles broke out here and there, shoving around the nets or discussions that lasted after lines changed.

The fans loved it. Hell, *I* loved it. If my man had been out there taking a beating, I might not have, but he was safely in the net. Although he too was a little more prone to shoving and using his stick to slap at Raptor players than usual. The first period was tight, not too many shots on goal but lots of end-to-end action with physicality galore. A fight was in the air. You could smell the simmering aggression as easily as you could smell popcorn popping, malty beer, and hamburgers frying.

So, when the fracas broke out along the boards to the left of Bryan, no one was surprised. We all might have leaped to our feet and cheered when big Adler Lockhart took a swing at equally big Petrov Egorov, a Raptor defenseman, after Egorov had gotten away with an uncalled slash on Lockhart. Bodies converged, and the fans went wild.

Of course, Tennant Rowe leaped into the melee in an attempt to pull one of the Raptors off one of his fellow Railers. What happened next occurred in a split second, but it was one of those sights that everyone who witnessed it would carry with them forever. Someone grabbed at Rowe's head in the mash of men and sticks and striped shirts. Later, on a thousand replays, we would see that the tug on Tennant's helmet was accidental. A Raptor just pawing at the horde and accidentally getting Ten's helmet. Off popped Rowe's skid lid, and into the mob flew Aarni Lankinen. Maybe I focused in on that fuckwit because of my in-depth knowledge of his abusive ways and his sick hatred of Tennant Rowe. Bryan had whispered things to me in the night. Things that made me start searching the *For Sale* ads in the papers for a trash truck. I yelled at Tennant to watch out. As if he could hear me over the other eighteen thousand rabid fans screaming for blood.

There's a saying about being careful what you wish for. When Lankinen reached Rowe, he slapped a hand to his shoulder and yanked him back over his extended leg. Rowe fell into the shuffling, punchy horde of skates, his head hitting the ice soundly, and he lay there. Unmoving, his head resting in an ever-increasing pool of blood, as skates danced around him.

The arena fell into silence. The Railers trainer flew over the boards and shoved his way through the men, who were only now seeing Rowe lying unconscious on the ice. I stood there high above the ice, paralyzed with fear. There was so much blood. And Rowe was not even twitching a finger. Bryan, bless his sweet and tender heart, raced out of the net and threw himself on Aarni's back, slamming his ex's face into the glass and pounding on his head.

No one cheered. Not one single person in that packed rink said a thing. I pushed through the worried fans, my heart in my throat, and barreled up the stairs. I had to get to the players' area and to Bryan. Of course, I wouldn't be allowed to sashay into the dressing room. Fuck. I spun and stared at the scene playing out on that massive screen. Players now back to their benches, a stretcher being taken out for Rowe, who was unmoving. And Aarni being escorted off the ice. Then the refs and linesmen stood in a small group by the timekeeper's table, discussing how many penalties would be handed out. Time in the sin bin was unimportant though.

Our star player was seriously injured. It seemed to take forever for them to get Tennant secured with a neck brace and gingerly lifted onto the stretcher. I had tried to see Jared from where I was seated, but he hadn't been on the bench. When the paramedics wheeled Ten through the Zamboni doors was when I saw Madsen, waiting for his man and taking his hand as they rushed the youngest Rowe boy out of the arena. I'd never seen a coach leave the game before, but then again Tennant and Jared weren't engaged in your typical coach/player relationship. God, Jared must have been a wreck.

Perhaps fifteen minutes had passed in deathly silence.

The rest of the game was a blur with a sickly loss for the Railers that no one would blame them for. How could a team return to playing full-bore when one of their most beloved friends was seriously injured?

It was a long, tense wait for Bryan. He and Stan exited together, heads close, and waved off the fans looking for an autograph. Erik followed Stan, his head down, and the rest of the team trickled out, none stopping for the fans this night.

"Hey," I said when Bryan broke away from Stan. The big Russian gave me a quick hug and then hustled to his car with his lover. "Any news?"

"They're saying it's bad."

"Fuck." I wanted to hug him but wasn't sure if we were doing that out and proud stuff. When he grabbed me and held me tightly to his chest, I embraced him back. No one would think anything of it tonight. Every player exiting that arena was hollow-eyed with grief and worry.

"He did that to Tennant because of me," Bryan gasped, his face buried in my neck.

"No, babe, no. He did that because he's a miserable excuse for a human being and a dirty weasel of a hockey player." My hands roamed over his back, patting and rubbing as he battled with tears. "You want to go to the hospital?"

"Yeah, please. If that's okay with you?"

Why was he asking that? "Of course you need to go."

"Sorry, yeah I want to go. You don't have to come. You can go home, and I'll call when we hear anything." He pulled back. "I just need to be with my team now."

I could see him beginning to shut down. Was it shock? Or was this more personal? He'd stepped away and wouldn't look me in the eyes. He was apologizing for not being with me, and I could see the fear in his expression.

"I'll come with you," I said with focused deter-mination.

"I won't be long," he said, and again he wouldn't meet my gaze.

What the hell? "Just thought you might like some company. I could fetch coffees and stuff." I ran out of words to explain how I really wanted to be with him and the team, and how I could be useful. Maybe it was my tone or the words themselves, but something must have reached him.

"Really?" he asked and finally looked at me.

Dieter brushed by. "I've got the room for two in the back," he announced, and I realized we weren't standing alone. We were in the middle of a scrum of players who all wanted to know about Ten, who all wanted to be at the hospital. Suddenly I was unsure. Maybe it wasn't my place to be there.

"But I can stay here if you think I'll be in the way."

Then the man I loved pushed back his shoulders, reacting to the uncertainty in my tone and becoming the confident person I know he could be.

"I *want* you there."

"Let's go."

He pressed a kiss to my cold cheek, and then we followed the procession of players and staff cars to Harris-burg University Hospital, which was *not* the official hospital of the Harrisburg Railers. We were headed to HUH because they had a state-of-the-art traumatic head injury unit.

I drove while Bryan whispered soft little prayers.

THIRTEEN

Bryan
      ————

Something had happened back at the arena. Familiar guilt had consumed me, and I didn't want to put Gatlin out, didn't want him to get angry with me, and I'd felt vulnerable and raw. Expressing his own concern, that he'd be in the way, was enough to pull me back, and god, I needed that. He wasn't Aarni. He was a man with a big heart who could see I was in distress.

I knew I was in shock. When I'd seen Aarni going after Ten, I couldn't move fast enough. I'd tried to get to Ten, wanted to help him.

I tried so hard.

But it was too late. Ten was lying still, with blood pooling under his head. I threw myself at Aarni, punched and kicked him, pulled his body out of the melee and onto the open ice.

I saw something in his eyes as my bare hands shoved at his helmet, delight at first and then fear as I hurt him. He'd tried to shove me off, calling me a bastard, telling me I was worthless, but fuck, I made that man bleed. I didn't know who pulled me away at first. I tried to fight them as well, but Stan's voice finally made me stop. He gripped my hands and turned me away from Aarni and Ten.

"*Dostatochno,*" he repeated over and over, staring right at me, his eyes bright with emotion, holding me until I finally relaxed into his hold. "*My ub'yem yego pozzhe,*" he added.

I don't know what he was saying, but I believed that whatever it was would mean Aarni would pay for what he'd done.

And now I was in this car, praying that Ten would be okay, unable to comprehend how something so stupid could have ended up with him in the hospital. Hockey was a dangerous sport, and there were often fights and scuffles. Guys coming away with split lips or bruised knuckles and grins.

Why had it all gone wrong for Ten?

The hospital came into view, and I immediately tensed at the sight of the press gathered around the gates. This was big news in our town; our superstar player bleeding out on the stark ice, playing on every phone and television, I'm sure.

A man I didn't recognize, wearing a Railers' hoodie, gestured for us to go to the left of the building, and I spotted Adler's sleek car ahead. We were being herded into a separate, private, parking lot, along with several other Railers' cars.

"Here," Layton Foxx said as soon as we stepped out. "You'll need these. Stay where you're put. No talking to the press, no social media, please. Wear the passes at all times, and if you have any questions…" His voice broke, and I could see the bright emotion in his eyes. He was a man who was supposed to guide this situation somehow, but above all that, he was Ten's friend. We all were. I wanted to say something to Layton to make it better, didn't want him to look so broken and fearful. I couldn't find a single thing that would work, not when I felt the same terrors I knew he had.

"It's okay," Gatlin offered, took the two passes, and put one around my neck. "I've got this."

Layton nodded his thanks, his knuckles white where he gripped the remaining passes.

"I don't know…" he began and then shook his head. "Shit."

Gatlin side-hugged him. "What can I do to help? Let me do this." He took the passes gently and then pushed both myself and Layton a little toward the door from the parking lot. "I've got this."

"Only team," Layton said, obviously torn with what he should be doing. His responsibility was to the team, but this was *Ten* hurt in there. "Loved ones," he added.

"Okay yeah, I assume someone called his family? His brothers?"

"Brady is on his way. Jamie is stuck in Florida but will be here in a few hours."

"And his parents?"

"On their way as well. We have a driver picking them up from the airport. Anyone who wants in that you don't know, call me, okay?"

"Will do."

Fear curled inside me at this question and answer conversation. Gatlin was so calm, but parents and siblings, that made everything so real. Layton looked from Gatlin to me and then strode into the hospital and vanished from view.

"I'm staying out here, Bryan, okay?"

"Huh?" I closed my eyes briefly and cursed my vision and the things I'd seen tonight. This could be it for Ten. Over. He had such a brilliant future ahead of him, and because of me, he'd been hurt. *I'm so cold. Why am I so cold?*

Gatlin cradled my face. "I'm staying here as point man," he said and moved his thumbs across my cheekbone briefly until I was aware and focused. "Is that okay with you?"

"What?"

"This is how I can help."

"Thank you. I think Layton needed to be in there. His team is…" *Fucked? Destroyed? Ten is the heart of this team. We're finished. Ten's finished—*

"Stop it, Bryan," Gatlin was firm. "That is your team as well. So whatever you're thinking. Stop it. You need to go in there and share this with your hockey family, and as soon as I can, I'll come in."

That fear inside became something else, a panic that I couldn't stop.

"I can't."

"Breath," Gatlin instructed. "In. Out."

I focused on his voice, and somehow, miraculously, the panic subsided. I reached up and gripped his hands.

"I love you," I said because it needed to be said at that moment.

"I love you, too," he replied, smiled at me and then gave me a gentle shove toward the door. There was a car at the barrier being let through. "This is me getting to work," he explained, and then, with a wink, he walked over to issue security passes.

When I got inside, an administrator showed me to a private room. The label on the door said *incident room*. I guess this was a place they used in emergencies, the only place for a large team of hockey players to sit and wait things out in private. I thanked him, entered and stood uncertainly, not knowing where to sit or wait. Should I go to Stan, as my fellow goalie? Was I good enough to stand with the forwards? Did I have friends here who needed me?

Then I saw the very thing I'd missed. There were no groups here. No one had their backs to me or to anyone else. There was a loose circle of men chatting softly. No one was angry; no one shouted. The circle widened a little, and Dieter gestured me in, so I stepped forward, and a couple of the guys nodded at me.

They wouldn't show any kind of compassion if they knew this was my fault. I should have told Ten that he was on Aarni's shit list. I should have said something to Jared…

"Way to go whaling on that asshole," Erik said and clapped me on the shoulder. "Stan said you were stuck to him like superglue, making that fucker bleed."

I smiled at Erik, as if that would stop him and anyone else talking, but no, I was coming off as the hero of the fucking hour, just for wanting to kill the man who'd made me so freaking fragile and needy.

When the fifth person told me the same thing, I snapped, and it wasn't pretty.

"It's my fault he went for Ten. He threatened him when Ten pulled him off me, and now Ten could be dying, so stop congratulating me for fucking everything up!" My words were staccato sharp and painful to say, and for a second everyone stared at me, a couple with their mouths open.

"What?" someone finally asked. I didn't know who, I couldn't tell, and I steeled myself for the anger.

Connor moved first, closing the door to the room and leaning on it. "Start from the beginning, Bryan."

I crossed my arms over my chest and tipped my chin to at least look like I had a backbone.

"It's my fault," I began again, but Connor held up a hand.

"Ten had to pull him off you?" He prompted, and I was lost for words.

"I let myself get into a stupid situation," I said, admitting to my part in it. "If I hadn't gone up on the roof, then Aarni wouldn't have had a chance to get in my face and try to… y'know."

"Wait, Aarni wanted to hurt you?" Connor asked as if I hadn't already explained everything once.

"That's irrelevant. It's my fault—"

"Enough," Connor snapped.

I winced and waited for a punch.

Stan pushed past the others and stood in front of me, blocking my view of Connor. "Not shouting at little B," he said, his stance wide. He was protecting me.

Me?

"I wasn't shouting at Bryan," Connor said, and he sounded a lot closer than the door, like he was actually right up in front of Stan. "Big Russian idiot, get out of my way," Connor added and then huffed as he pushed Stan to one side. Stan moved a little, but not all the way, and he looked fierce when I caught his expression. A warmth bloomed inside but vanished when I saw how close Connor was. Abruptly face-to-face with the captain of the Railers, I didn't know what the hell to say. Seemed I didn't need to say anything and that Connor had all the words.

"You don't deserve any kind of evil shit that Aarni had going on. Anyone of us walking in on Aarni causing trouble would have defended you or stood by your side if you needed us. This has nothing to do with you, and everything to do with Ten. What I see here is premeditation from Aarni to hurt Ten, a threat he carried out, so I need to know exactly what he said. To you and to Ten."

"Here?" I asked, glancing around at the Railers, who all looked as pissed as Connor did.

Connor was suddenly embarrassed. "Shit, no, of course not. We can go somewhere quiet."

This was the moment. I could go two ways from here, not tell my story, and no one would ever know anything, or I could just get everything off my chest.

I don't know how I actually managed to stop talking once I started. I had so much to say, and it poured out until there was nothing left. When I finished, I heard a noise at the door. Gatlin was standing there with an understanding expression. We stared at each other for a long moment, and then Gatlin cleared his throat, causing everyone to look at him.

"Sorry to interrupt, guys, but Brady is ten minutes away."

Boston had been playing Pittsburgh, less than four hours by car, but it hadn't been that long, had it? Maybe they'd let him use the jet. I mean, how bad was this injury?

Abruptly the room fell quiet and respectful. Brady would be walking into this group of men who hadn't managed to stop his little brother being hurt. He'd be devastated and furious.

We drifted back to the chairs in small clusters around the room, and I ended up sitting with Stan and Erik.

"What did you say to me on the ice," I asked after a moment's silent contemplation of everything. Stan looked up at me with a blank expression. "When I was hitting Aarni," I explained.

Stan stiffened at the name, and Erik placed a hand on his knee. I'm not sure that was enough for the big Russian to back down though because there was a flash of anger in his eyes.

"We make kill later," he said and then laced his fingers with Erik's. "Aarni, we make dead him, after this day."

I'm sure that Stan was talking rhetorically, but who knew with the big, bad Russian.

"Stan tried to get into the Raptors' locker room," Adler said from behind me.

"I'm kill," Stan said, and there was no way he was being dissuaded.

Was it wrong to admit that the words Stan spoke, low, gruff, and utterly certain, made me think that Aarni would somehow pay for what he'd done to Ten? We hadn't heard a thing about what had happened to Aarni, not after he'd been removed from the ice.

"Connor got in his way, a human-captain barrier against Stan's temper." Adler knocked elbows with me. "He's a brave man. I wouldn't get in between Stan and someone who had hurt a loved one."

The door opened, and Coach Benning stepped into our private area. Everyone stood, and he raised a hand to quiet any questions.

"He's comfortable," was all he said.

Every one of us had to have the same question. What kind of bullshit summary was that? Was Ten badly hurt? Was he dying? Would he play hockey again?

We didn't have a chance to say a thing or ask any questions when Gatlin arrived back at the door, along with Brady Rowe. The oldest Rowe brother was the captain of Boston, had seen so much in his time, the same as other players in their thirties. He was calm, but the pain and fear in his eyes made my heart hurt.

They ushered him through, and we all sat again. Jamie would arrive in a few hours, and then their parents. We would be sitting here waiting and praying. We had a game in two days, at home, Buffalo in town, but all I could think was that Ten's blood was mixed into the ice in a way that no skater ever wanted to see again.

. . .

WE SAT THERE for most of the night. Jamie arrived and hurried past, and a little later, Ten's parents were there, his mom red-eyed but stoic, his dad pale. Only when they went in did Jared come out.

We hadn't seen him in all the hours we'd been at the hospital, and I imagined he'd been by Ten's side for as long as he could be. Stan and Connor walked up to him immediately, screening him from the rest of us. Then they stepped back. Jared took a long drink from a water bottle, and after a few moments, he began to haltingly explain everything.

"He's awake some of the time; that's a good sign. He has a skull fracture from falling at an angle. He uhmmm…" Jared swallowed and then cleared his throat. "He can't talk and can't move his left arm, has a contusion…" Jared tapped at his head, "… blood on the brain, and a skate caught him here." This time he drew a finger from ear to throat. "That accounts for the blood they think…it was very close…" His voice broke, and for a second, he bent over with his hands on his knees, his breathing ragged.

"You want to sit down?" Connor asked and pressed a hand to his shoulder.

"No… I need to get back in. I just wanted… It was important to tell you all." He took a moment to corral his wild breathing. "It missed his external carotid artery by a millimeter. Just one small breath difference. There's nothing anyone can do but wait. You can all go home. I promise I'll call someone to pass on messages."

None of us wanted to leave. Stan sat stubbornly on the seat, and he was the only one who wouldn't do what the coaches and Connor wanted. They said we should go. Stan wasn't budging, although Erik had to leave for Noah. So I sat with Stan, and no amount of cajoling or ordering was moving the two weird goalies.

No sir, no way. I was Stan's backup, and this was where I belonged.

If that meant that Buffalo scored on us a hundred times in the next game because we were exhausted, then so be it.

Of course, everyone in management, trying to be responsible, was pissed at us. But, we were there when his parents came out with Jamie and Brady, and we got them coffee and sat with them until they went back in. We were useful.

Jared didn't come out once.

"I hate this," Brady muttered on his last walk out of the room. He kicked at the nearest table and then the door, and finally, he picked up a chair and threw it at the wall. Only when he'd thrown his third chair did Stan intervene, gripping his arms and letting the oldest Rowe brother cry.

When they separated, not one of us said a thing. We would take this single moment to the grave with us. Hockey players don't cry. They get hurt, they stand right back up, there's blood on the ice, you scrape it away, and you carry the fuck on.

So we would never tell anyone that Brady Rowe, captain of a hockey team, cried in Stan's arms or that Stan joined in with the grief for his best friend.

Nor that I watched them and cried with them.

WE SAW Ten at a little after nine a.m. Jared needed to talk to management, and he wanted Stan to get a chance to see Ten. That was all. I never expected to be able to go in as well, but Stan tugged at my arm and wouldn't leave me alone. He was talking to me in Russian and refused to release me.

Stepping inside Ten's room, I didn't know what to expect. Wires, tubes, his mouth covered with a guard possibly, at least a combination of all the horrors I'd seen on television. But he was actually peaceful and seemed to be merely sleeping.

Stan hip-checked me closer to the bed, and we were finally next to Ten, and as if he knew we were there, he opened his eyes, and there was recognition in their green depths. There were bandages on his throat, and they'd shaved some of his hair, and fuck, he was white, but the essence of Ten was still there and still focused.

Stan patted Ten's chest. "Is much okay, am kill Lankinen."

Ten's eyes widened, and I shoved at Stan. "We're not killing anyone."

When Stan subsided into silence, I didn't know what to say next, and a small awkward part of me wanted to fill the quiet. "I'm sorry that he hurt you. It was all my fault."

At first, Ten appeared frustrated with his inability to talk. Then he raised his hand and gripped mine, and he held it so tight and frowned up at me. He shook his head a little and winced, and I squeezed his hand and then extricated myself from his firm hockey grip. His other arm lay useless on the bed, and I remembered Jared said that Ten couldn't move it.

Jared came back into the room, and we quietly left, but as I glanced back at Jared pressing a soft kiss on Ten's forehead, that familiar terror hit me. What if this was Ten done? What if the man they dubbed a future Hall of Famer, a champion, was done? How could he live the rest of his life without hockey?

Life was so damn short, so why was I wasting it being

so fucking scared of myself and the world around me. I'm a freaking tough hockey player, and my life so far had been a mess of insecurity and stupid situations.

I am going to channel the fuck out of my inner hero, and I am going to be the best man I can be.

First of all, though, I really need to find Gatlin. Because I really wanted to be with him when it was my turn to cry.

FOURTEEN

Gatlin

S o many tears…
The past couple of days had been like walking through a *Silent Hill* game. Our lives had become gray and foggy, filled with demons that lurked out of sight, dragging massive swords on metal floors, the sound coming closer and closer, death right around every murky corner. I'd come awake from that particular nightmare a few times, usually at Fuck-Me-o'clock, to find Bryan either tossing and turning or gone from my bed. This time, the horrors woke me at five a.m., and my man was at my side, sleeping peacefully.

I rolled over and touched him, his face, his ear, his eyebrow. Wound in slumber, Bryan wrinkled his nose, so I stopped and just let my hand drift over his chest and stomach. Palm over his navel, the scent of him all over me and the bed, I studied his chest rising and falling.

"We have a game tonight," Bryan murmured groggily, pulling my gaze from his chest to his face. His eyelids were heavy and his hair flat to one side of his head. "I can't even think about hockey right now."

I leaned down to drop a kiss to his shoulder, right beside a small birthmark. He moved a bit, a slow ripple of muscle that reminded me of a snake, the movement starting at his neck and rolling downward, moving his body in a sinuous, undulating way.

"Bryan…" I said, the sensation of him moving against me stirring up desires that had no place in a mood such as the one we'd been trapped in.

"Nothing is right," he said, wrapping his fingers around my wrist and leading my hand to his cock, the sheets smooth and cool brushing the back of my hand. "Nothing is good right now. The team is lost, Jared is on an extended leave, the league is investigating Aarni, and that will lead them to me. I'll have to talk to the league about us…tell them how I let him…" He drew in a shaky breath, his hand wrapping mine around his dick. My cock began to fatten up despite my mind chiding it to stop. "Ten is so bad, and nothing is right. But this? You and me? This is the only right and good thing I have right now. Can you love me just a little? Show me there's light and good?"

"Of course," I whispered, covering his mouth with mine as we stroked him slowly. His hand fell to the bed. I pulled the covers off to expose his body. Then, I touched and kissed, sucking when he asked and stopping when it was too much. His hips punched upward with each brush of my fingers. I worked my way down until I had his erection in my mouth. Bryan groaned, his fingers ripping the bottom sheet off the mattress so quickly the elastic snapped. Pleasuring him, I kind of found myself stepping out of the terrors of the injury to our friend. With his balls on my tongue and my hand working him, we left the darkness behind, if just for a short while. I sucked on his nuts, eyes closed in bliss, then licked a sloppy path back to his cock. He lifted his ass from the bed.

"Gatlin...suck hard. Get me off. Get me off."

That breathy plea nearly ended me. I released my hand from his dick, then sucked him down my throat, my free hand cupping his wet balls, tugging and rolling as he writhed and shouted. He came with a hard thrust that made my eyes water. Hot spunk coated my throat. Swallowing rapidly, moving my hand to my own cock, I sucked him even harder and faster, getting a yelp of pure bliss out of the man that kicked off my own orgasm. I shot all over his thigh, his cock sliding from between my lips, leaving a thin slick of cum over my lower lip. Bucking like a bronco, I fisted myself even harder, each shudder intense.

"Ah, shit," I coughed, my palm gliding over the head of my cock, making the tremors start again.

"Thank you," I heard him say before he tugged on my head, his grip firm on my jaw, and led me to his mouth. He heaved me onto my back, long legs knotting up with mine, his hip flush to mine, his tongue probing deep. When the kiss ended, he hoisted himself up, both arms locked, his hands on either side of my head. "Thank you for that little bit of right."

"No need to thank me." I reached up to cup his face. "I want to give you all the right a man can give another man. Whenever you need it."

"I love you."

"And I love you. Now go shower and do hockey. Tennant would not want his team to give up simply because he's been sidelined for a bit."

We all knew that Ten was not out for a bit. We all knew that Tennant Rowe had a long and arduous journey ahead. We also knew that Tennant Rowe was a fighter.

Bryan blinked a few times, stole another kiss, and then left our bed, his body flushed with sex. As he padded off to shower and get ready for the morning skate, my gaze latched onto the tattoo on his lower back. There was no ugly there now, only art, beauty, color, and light. I sprang from the bed, as well as a man my age could spring, and grabbed my sketchpad and my colored pencils from the dresser. Then I called a few people until I was put into contact with Brady Rowe.

AFTER BRYAN TOOK OFF, I did as well. My first appointment wasn't until two, perks of owning your own shop, so I drove to the hospital, backpack filled with pencils, pens, and a new sketchpad filled with new ideas. I had no clue if I could even get in to see Tennant, but I had to try. If his family let me in and if he couldn't talk yet, I'd even brought the bell from the counter. He could ding once for yes and twice for no. If that didn't work, I'd just write the letters down on paper and recite the alphabet, and he could ding on the right letter until we spelled something out. Hey, it worked on *Breaking Bad* so it would work for us.

My plans hit a small snag when I ran into a security guard sitting outside Tennant's room. This was new. Probably some asshole sports blogger or fan had tried to sneak in to see or talk or take a picture of Ten in his hospital bed. Nothing would surprise me. When I approached the man in the dark suit and even darker shades, I paused a foot away in case he had a taser. I wasn't exactly the most reputable-looking person with my scruffy face, ripped jeans, shitkickers, and *Sons of Anarchy – Redwood Original* T-shirt under a hand-painted Led Zeppelin denim jacket. The inkwork sneaking out of my sleeves and the collar of my shirt probably added to my classy look.

He rose from his folding chair and stared down at me. Then he spoke. Whatever he was saying, it was not in

English. I suspected it was Russian. The man was the size of a bull elephant, and his bald head gleamed under the fluorescent lights. I'd heard Stan mention that he "knew people" but never suspected that he really "knew people" who would sooner carve out your spleen with a rusty butter knife than look at you.

"Blah-blah-blah-blah-blah. Go away now."

I hefted my backpack a little higher on my shoulder, ready to engage in verbal war when someone called my name from behind me. I glanced back and saw Ryker, Jared's son, walking toward us with a tray filled with large coffee cups.

"He's cool. We know him," Ryker, who apparently had been run over a few times by Mr. Angry Pachyderm here, told the security person/bodyguard/terrifying human being.

"*Da*." The man sat back down and returned to staring holes into the wall.

"He's someone Stan knows. We gave up asking how," Ryker informed me, using his hip to nudge at the door.

I hustled around him and pushed the door into the private room open. "Thanks." Yeah, the kid was exhausted. You could tell by his weary tone and the bags under his eyes.

"Dad, Ten, look who Igor was intimidating."

I slipped in on Ryker's heels, feeling terribly out of place. Jared was seated beside Tennant in an ugly orange chair, his face thick with whiskers, his eyes as tired as Ryker's were. Ten was still a mass of tubes and wires, but his eyes, those bright green eyes, were alert.

"Yo," Tennant croaked after a full moment had passed. Jared's smile was brilliant.

"Hey, you're talking. That's awesome. I probably shouldn't have come, but I kind of had this idea…"

"Don't be silly. Sit down here." Jared stood slowly, groaning as his back popped several times. "I need to walk a bit." Jared brushed a tender kiss to Tennant's brow. Then Ryker handed his father a cup of coffee before he left. I stood at the end of the bed; the white walls and bedding glaringly bright.

"Only two people allowed in here at a time," Ryker informed me, then flopped into another, equally ugly, chair in the corner. The window was open, the blinds casting strips of bright sunlight on the man lying amid all that technology and white bedding.

"Shit, I didn't realize. I should go and let Jared be here."

"No, really, it's cool. He needs to get up and move." Ryker said, then yawned into his coffee.

"Cool," Tennant added to the conversation. I looked from Ryker to Ten. "Happy…see…you."

"I'm happy to see you too. Look, I uh, I won't take up much time. I'm sure your parents and brothers are going to be here soon."

Tennant nodded and then grimaced. Ryker sat up sharply when Ten winced, then relaxed back into his seat when the pain eased off Ten's young face.

"Mom…cookies."

That made me smile. I recalled my mother's cookies and how when I'd been a child, and in need of comfort, they always made me feel better. Sometimes I missed my parents terribly.

"Then I'll be quick." I shrugged off my backpack and dug into it, extracting my sketchpad, then walked closer to Ten. The machines he was attached to beeped steadily. "Not sure if you know this, but Bryan has a nasty scar on his back from a fall through some glass."

"Inked…it."

I nodded at Ten. "Yeah, we did ink it. And we made something he felt was ugly into something beautiful. When you're better, I think we can do something for your neck." I glanced at the thick white gauze wrapped around his throat. My mind dredged up Jared's words the night of the injury as I stared at those sterile bandages and tape. One millimeter to the side and Ten might have bled out. Time was so short with those we loved. Life was just a fucking crapshoot, so play the game all out, right? "I spoke with your brother Brady, who's quite the family historian. He informed me that your family dates back to the days of the Norman conquest of England. According to Brady, the early Rowe's held a family seat in Norfolk, which was a gift from a duke for their allegiance in the Battle of Hastings." I paused to see if Ten was growing tired yet, but he seemed alert, so I carried on.

"Brady sent me an image of a coat of arms for the Rowe family. The central animal of the Rowe coat of arms is a lion, which is a symbol of courage, bravery, strength, valor, stateliness, and nobility. All attributes that you have and will show to the world as you battle back from this injury. So, if you're into all of this so far, I thought we could ink a golden lion over that scar. This one…" I flipped the page to show him the sketch of a lion from the Middle Ages, "is a close interpretation of the one on your family coat of arms. I've just drawn him standing on his rear legs brandishing a sword because, let's face it, a lion wearing a crown and swinging a big ass sword in the air is just fucking cool."

Both young men grunted in agreement.

"With him upright, he'll cover the scar completely. What do you think?"

Tennant's emerald eyes flared.

"Dude," he groaned, and I wasn't sure if that meant he was happy or in pain or what.

"Do you need the nurse?"

He shook his head gingerly and smiled. Ryker sat up, coffee in hand, and echoed Ten's "dude" comment.

"I can do something else…" I tried to flip the sketchpad shut, but Tennant grunted at me.

"Give it…here," he said, his words still slow and slurred.

Ryker took the page after I tore it from the pad. "We will totally be in to get inked as soon as he's able. Yeah, Ten?"

The reply was slow to come, but the "Totes" from Tennant was worth the wait.

I PASSED Mr. and Mrs. Rowe on the way out of Tennant's room. True to her word, Tennant's mother had a tin in her hands. Igor never stopped me as I left, which was beyond unsettling. Hoisting my backpack higher on my shoulder after a fast trip to the bathroom, I came upon Jared and Ryker huddled together in an alcove by a soda machine, their conversation floating down the still corridor. They must've vacated so Ten's folks could be with him for a bit.

"…isn't happening. I can't get my head around this." Ryker coughed. The kid *had* looked more than a little shell-shocked. "Dad, what the fuck will Ten do without hockey?"

"Okay, no one has said anything about him not being able to play again, and we're not going to allow that kind of thinking to enter our minds." Jared cupped the back of his son's head lovingly but firmly.

"Yeah, right, okay. I know, sorry. I just…this is freaking me out. I sit there and look at him…I have to go play for that team when I graduate. Dad, I hate the thought of being a future Raptor. Why was it that fucking team that drafted me? I just…this whole thing is fucked. I was so excited to be picked up and now…"

"I know. We'll worry about later. Right now, we focus on Ten, right?"

I lowered my head and lifted a shoulder to make myself invisible. Not that I had to worry about being seen. Jared and Ryker were hugging each other and oblivious to one inked-up dude passing by.

I DROVE HOME, eager to grab a bite to eat and then get to work.

My brother and Jess were sitting on the couch when I ambled into the shop, having what seemed like a tea party. I quirked an eyebrow at them and the teapot on the floor as I made my way to the fridge under the counter to see if there was anything not moldering inside that I could eat.

"I ate the chicken that was in there," Jess called out. I closed the door, straightened, and gave her a dirty look which she smirked at me. "It was dry. I did you a favor."

"Right. So, who is who?" I asked, leaning on the glass counter as I eyed my relatives. "Obviously Jess is the Mad Hatter." She tapped the pink top hat on her head. It matched her pink skirt and black shirt well. Garrett checked his watch. "And you're the White Rabbit."

"Said the March Hare," my brother replied, then took a sip of tea.

"Ha." I left them to their tea and chitchat and went into my workspace, stomach rumbling, and sat at my desk. A craving for sugar cookies with frosting overwhelmed me. My gaze moved over the stuff on my desk, the bills and the books, the sketches and ideas, an empty coffee mug and a spattering of pencils, old and new. My glasses lay beside my laptop, which solved one question. And back in the corner, shoved behind several issues of a monthly magazine for tattoo artists and a box of tissues, was a picture of my family.

I nudged the tissues aside, pulled the picture over the magazines and studied it. Mom, Dad, Garret, who was a teenager, me and Gina. Gina was just a toddler. She was seated on Mom's lap, and us boys were on either side of my mother, with Dad directly behind her.

Things had been good then. Before Gina had died. Back when they'd still loved their middle child. If I was sick like Tennant, would they come to see me? Would she bake those cookies with the sugary frosting? Would they sit by my side? Would they forgive me? If I asked, would they forgive me for letting my sister die alone?

My phone was in my hand. I don't recall dialing, but I must have because it was ringing, and then…then my mother was asking who was calling.

"Mom." The word was gritty and thick. I sounded like Tennant, forcing each thought into a word that I hoped I could pronounce properly. "It's me…Gatlin."

"Gatlin." I waited for something, not sure what. "It's been so long. Why did you stop calling? We've been worried. Is your brother okay?"

"Yeah, uh, yeah, Mom. We're both fine." I spun around in my chair, and there he stood, in the doorway, his face set, so no emotion was showing. Typical Garrett. "We're fine. Is Dad okay?"

"Yes, he's fine. He's outside puttering."

That made me smile and tear up, but mostly smile. Puttering. A word only a mother would use.

"Mom, if I were sick in the hospital, would you bring me sugar cookies?"

Garrett's brow furrowed like a newly worked field.

"The ones with the frosting?"

"Yeah, those."

"Of course. Are you sick?"

"No, I'm not sick just…I'm sorry about Gina, Mom." It sort of tumbled out of me, as toast crumbs that flitter from your lips to your shirt. "I know you and Dad blame me."

A long silence on the other end. I blinked at the tears. Garrett's eyebrows were set into a deep "V."

"No, Gatlin, we were wrong to take it out on you. We know it wasn't your fault." And then she began to cry. "We miss you boys, more than you will ever know. I'm sorry for making you…"

And then she kind of broke down, and I had nothing to say because I'd never planned for this. Calling her had been a wild spur of the moment sort of lunacy, brought on by the Rowe's and their adoration for their youngest son.

"She misses us." I coughed as my mother worked out her stuff on the other end of the line. "And she's sorry."

Garrett's face went blank. That was exactly how I felt. "Well, that's a start."

Yes, yes it was.

FIFTEEN

Bryan

The game was a mess. We'd started out with the best of intentions, but we learned the hardest lesson of our careers that night. We relied too much on Ten, and with him not there, we were an unfocused mess. The team was too emotionally vulnerable and losing Ten was losing the heart of us.

With absolute focus, Stan had led us out, cries of "For Ten" echoing in the locker room as we left. If the words were forced, if the intention was muddied by our worries, then we ignored it all.

We could do this, we could go out as a team, and we could take a win tonight without Ten. Our focus was filling that gap, closing ranks, holding a steady course.

But Stan wasn't in the right headspace. He cracked his stick over the net halfway through the second period, after letting in four goals. I hoped to God Coach didn't put me in, and after a heated debate with a determined Stan and with the score at four-nothing, I think Coach thought it didn't matter. Or maybe that it mattered to Stan too much, and he didn't call for me to replace him. I think he saw that Stan needed to work out his aggression, and the rest of the team pulled together a little more to have the game finally and painfully ending at the same score, four to nothing.

We only had two more days to get our heads around what had happened, and to play hockey the right way, but how we would get there, I didn't know.

The crowd was subdued as well, a lot of signs with Ten's name on them, some tearful interviews on social media, and of course the big one, Jared missing from the bench.

Then there was that demonstration outside, the one that had started way before we'd arrived for the game. Some church using what had happened to Ten as proof that God hated gays. That's exactly what the signs said. I wanted to go over there and tear them out of their hands. Ten wasn't *just* a hockey player. He wasn't *just* gay. Those things didn't define him. He was a human, and they were stripping that humanity from him. Stan actually walked their way, but Pete, our security guy, was a brick wall, and he used his words to get Stan to listen to him.

They weren't there when the game ended because there'd been trouble, loyal Railers' fans, and even fans of the opposing team, causing a scuffle which ended up with the police dispersing the crowd. Of course, that didn't stop the waiting TV crews capturing it all, which meant the headlines changed from 'injured hockey player' to 'injured openly gay hockey player' in an instant.

"You can talk to me if you want," Gatlin murmured. He was the big spoon to my little spoon, curving around me, his hand over my waist, his breath tickling my neck with every exhale. We'd been lying like this since I'd come home to his place. He'd taken one look at me and encouraged me into bed, and he hadn't asked me one question or demanded I explain why I was so quiet.

"I wouldn't know what to say," I replied from the heart.

He pressed a kiss to my neck and snuggled closer, drawing the blanket right up around my throat.

"I'll be here when you do," he murmured.

I was happy here, far away from the hateful mobs who wanted me and others like me to burn in hell, safe from having to consider that the Railers were broken right now. My eyes burned, and my chest ached, and I didn't know if I wanted to cry or scream or rail at the unfairness of what had happened. The outlook wasn't good. There wasn't only a skull fracture which had caused internal bleeding, but there was swelling pressing on his spine. He'd lost the feeling in his legs, and no one could say when he would be out of the hospital.

"Can we go and see Ten?" I asked, twisting in his hold until I faced him.

"Always." He sounded confused, maybe thinking why I would be asking something like that.

"Now. I mean, like, right now. I know Jared isn't sleeping, and he's there, and I'd like to take him something, coffee, food, anything." I realized I sounded on edge and more than a little desperate but watching the Railers fall apart tonight and still feeling as if this was all my fault, I *needed* to be doing something to scratch away the terrors in my mind.

To his credit, Gatlin never blinked. He kissed my nose, a small kiss, nothing but a reminder of what I was to him, and then he slid out from under the blanket. Only when he had his jeans on did he turn to face me, realizing I was still in bed.

"Now is fine, Bryan," he said.

Had I been waiting for him to say that? Did I need his

permission? Jesus, how fucked up was I? Dressed, he headed to find jackets and keys, and all too soon we were at McDonald's drive-through, picking up food and coffees. Because of media attention and the increased risk, this morning they'd moved Ten to a private space with security. I didn't know the two guards, but they recognized me.

Even so, they couldn't let me in. They said I was on the approved list, but at midnight, it was protocol not to let anyone in.

"It's okay," I said, "I just wanted to—"

"Bryan, Gatlin," Jared said from behind the guards, coming out of the hospital, rubbing at his eyes. "What's wrong?"

"We should be asking you that," I blurted out and thrust the bag of burgers at him. He took the bag, and I handed him the coffee, so he was juggling everything. "Sorry," I apologized and went to take it back, and the coffee slipped from our joint hold. Only Gatlin scrambling for it saved the situation from being an unmitigated disaster. *I'm so fucking clumsy.*

I was shaking inside, and Jared stared at me as if I was an idiot, or was he confused?

"Come and join me? Everyone else has gone home, although Ten's mom only just left. The doc was here earlier, and I think I'm processing what they told me, but I feel shaky, although I'm not sure I've eaten; maybe not at all today. I needed some air, but I would really like it if someone would sit and talk to me and tell me..." He stopped and shook his head. "Sorry, I'm rambling."

He couldn't recall eating? Also, I wondered how much sleep he'd had since the accident. He was gaunt and hunched in on himself, not the strong man who could make a line of defensemen quake in their skates. Then it hit me. He needed someone else to be strong for him right at this moment. Not a neurotic guilt-ridden kid, but a man, and with Gatlin at my side, I could be that person. I felt it deeply, and it was like a fire in my veins.

"We'd love to join you," I said, and Gatlin nudged my arm. I like to think he was proud of me. Hell, *I* was proud of myself.

We followed him past the guards, who issued us badges and ushered us into a small anteroom with a table and some chairs. The walls were a soft cream, with paintings on each of them and windows that faced a private garden area. It was illuminated from the light in the room facing it, which was a small kitchen of sorts. Jared slid into the nearest sofa that faced the door, and I watched as he relaxed inch by inch into the soft cushions. He placed the bag of food next to him and fell on the coffee as if he needed caffeine more than air.

"I think he should eat," I said to Gatlin, who nodded. In a smooth move worthy of Ten himself, I managed to wrangle the coffee from Jared and rummaged inside the McDonald's bag for a cheeseburger. "Eat," I demanded.

For a moment I thought Jared was going to argue with me, but then he took the wrapped food and peeled back the paper. He bit into it as if he was worried it was poisoned, but after chewing for a second, he carried on, swallowed, and proceeded to eat that burger and the other we'd added just in case. Then the nuggets, then the fries. Until the bag was empty. He interspersed the whole burger-fest with slurps of coffee, and finally, he sat back on the sofa and closed his eyes.

"So they released the pressure on the bleed, and the feeling is coming back in Ten's legs," Jared said after a moment of peace.

Hope flared inside me. "That's a good thing, right?" I sat next to Jared on the sofa, "Right?"

Jared opened his eyes, and they were bright with emotion. "Yes. Rehab, therapy, fuck knows what, but he'll get up out of that bed under his own steam."

I don't think I'd ever felt lighter. Ten was coming back. "He'll be on skates in no time." I was sure of it.

Jared nodded slowly, but there was no answering smile. "He still can't talk properly, and sometimes when he's trying to say simple things, he falters. The damage might be too severe to skate again. No one knows."

I reached out to Jared then, placed a hand on his knee briefly. "Ten is young; he's a fighter." I glanced at Gatlin, who smiled encouragingly. "I'm convinced he'll be back soon."

Jared also smiled, although it didn't quite reach his eyes. "The cops were here today," he said, so softly I had to strain to hear.

They'd taken a statement from me, about what happened on the roof, about the kind of man I thought Aarni Lankinen was, but who knew what would happen next.

"About what happened on the ice?"

"The VT is ambiguous, doesn't show if Aarni hurt Ten worse, doesn't matter if he'd threatened Ten. In their words, it's hockey."

"Jesus."

"I get that. I just don't know how I'm going to…" He scrubbed at his eyes. "Look, do me a favor, pass the word about the op to the team, let people know. I'm all done with telling the same story over and over."

I typed a message into the group chat but showed Jared before I hit send.

Ten's op went well. He has feeling in his legs.

I wanted to add that this was fantastic news, that I was filled with hope, and that Jared had eaten burgers. Also that the cops had been to see Ten. I didn't. I just waited for Jared to nod that the message was acceptable, and then pressed send. The Aarni part wasn't my story to tell, and there was enough shit out there at the moment without pouring more fuel onto the flames.

Aarni hadn't played with the Raptors tonight; he'd been a healthy scratch. Whether that was team punishment or not, I didn't know. Both Canadian and US papers were headlining the hit in their sports pages, and I know that if we had been up there now, reporters would be camped out at the hotel. Ten was the new generation of players, and he had star potential. It seemed as though everyone was invested in his recovery, even outside the close community of hockey.

But there was peace here, and I was glad of it.

Jared stood and stretched tall, then screwed up the wrappers and the bag and tossed them into the trash.

"Thank you," he said as he reached the door. "I needed this."

"No worries," I offered as Gatlin took my hand and laced our fingers. "Food is always a good thing."

Jared huffed a soft laugh. "I'm not thanking you just for the food, Bryan. Never just for the food."

WE WERE IN WASHINGTON, with a game in less than eight hours, when the news came down from on high that Aarni had been given a league suspension of five games. When the announcement from the National Hockey League's Player Safety Department hit after morning practice, with Coach Benning reading from the press release, the mood in the locker room went from tired and pissed to furious.

"Five," Adler repeated and threw his gloves into his cubby. "Jesus, did they not see what he did?"

"There's more," Coach continued, holding up his hand to quiet us and continued reading the NHL missive. "Lankinen has added his own release."

"Fucking asshole," Connor snapped.

"I'm kill," Stan shouted as he stood with clenched fists. I wanted to stand next to him and pledge my allegiance to any killing. Five games were nothing.

Coach waited for us to quiet again. "This was more than a careless and reckless action on my part. It was senseless. Tennant Rowe was openly vulnerable, and the situation was one in which I realize I let my emotions get the better of me. I am in contact with the Rowe family. I have decided to accept the NHL's decision and will not be appealing it. I have no further comment regarding this matter."

The noise was deafening, a cacophony of cursing and threats and for the longest time Coach let us vent.

Erik stood in front of Stan, a hand on his chest, talking to him, and Stan's expression was fierce and determined. I watched Connor stand silently in the middle of the room, his hands clenched into fists. And me? The guilt was there, Ten and I should have said something before about the roof. Then maybe we could have stopped this? One by one we fell quiet until finally every single one of us was back in our allotted cubby space and all eyes were on Coach. Now what?

"The game tonight," he began. "If Brady and Jamie Rowe can be back today playing for their teams, we can pull our shit together for Ten. All of us. Ten does not define our team, we have a whole room of talent here, and we need to shake this shit off, whether we like it or not. If Ten were here, he'd be saying this, and you know it."

Skaters murmured their assent and then went silent.

"Okay then. Washington is a strong, determined team, and they will bring their A game. Go home, get you pregame nap, get your carbs, find your lucky whatever the hell it is, do your rituals, and come back with the intention of playing Railers hockey the right way."

He didn't wait for agreement. He just left, the other coaches slipping out after him and closing the door. We were alone, and all eyes went to Connor.

He turned his gaze to the ceiling briefly and then sighed. "I want to hurt that man for what he did to Ten. I felt as if our team was destroyed that night. I thought it was all over. What was the point." He paused, but no one interjected. He couldn't be standing there just telling us that he thought we were done. He crossed his arms over his chest. "The point is we're still a team, and losing Ten hurts, but we can close ranks here. Charlie, I know you're in a shit position of centering Ten's line, but it's not his line while he's not here; it's yours."

"Yes, boss," Martin "Charlie" Brown said. He'd centered the fourth line for so long that going up to first against the best D-men that other teams had, was always going to be hard.

"D's we need to tighten up in front of the net. Wings, we have gaps on all four lines that we need to fill, and Gids?"

Gideon "Gids" Levesque looked up, startled. Poor guy had been called up from the Rush to cover the hole in our fourth line with everyone else being moved around. No one wanted to fill that space when the reason for it was so shit. He had the expression of a permanently frightened rabbit, but his play, at least, had been more consistent in the last game than the rest of us.

"Captain?"

"It's shit why you're here, but you deserve the place, and last game you were solid. Keep it up."

Gids sat upright, his shoulders back, "Yes, Cap."

"Stan, Bryan, you're our last defense here, you stop those pucks if they get through. Stan, you need to rein it in for me, buddy."

Stan muttered in Russian and then sighed noisily. "I'm catch all pucks. I'm show true grit," he said, and there was absolute focus and determination mixed into his angry expression.

"What Stan said," I offered after him. A few of the guys laughed at that, which lightened the tone a little and allowed Connor to uncross his arms and relax a little.

"Okay," Connor said and rubbed his hands, "Sleep, carb, rituals, lucky shit, back here to take down Washington. Agreed?"

I WAS backup in the Washington game, able to watch the division matchup with a dispassionate eye. We played well, focused, not temper-driven, not listless and wrecked. There were some signs held up at the glass, but not one of them spouted hate. What there was made absolute sense to me. The fans were closing ranks around us, holding us near and helping us in ways they would never understand, and there were more than a few people in Railers blue jerseys in the seats.

I knew precisely where Gatlin was sitting, and I skated right up to the glass and caught his eye, tapping the glass with my stick and blowing him a kiss. He caught the kiss in a comically exaggerated fashion and pretended to place it into his pocket.

I was so in love with that man it was ridiculous.

The game was hard, but we were tied after two periods, one goal apiece. Gids got his first NHL goal only a few seconds into the last period, off a beautiful face-off win at the Washington end. It was poetry to watch, and when Gids passed me and bumped fists, he was whooping in joy. We held that lead by the skin of our teeth, and when the buzzer sounded, we were done. We'd won.

I think we needed that.

For the forward guys stepping up. For Gids with his first NHL goal. For Jared and his D-men. For the coaches who had watched us begin to implode and prayed we got out of it, and for the fans who deserved the win.

But mostly for Ten.

SIXTEEN

Gatlin

B ryan and I did this half-assed job of decorating my space above the shop for Christmas. He hung some tinsel, and we grabbed a fake tree, already decorated with gold candy canes, tiny plastic golden balls and really gross gold glitter-encrusted gingerbread men. Neither of us felt much like celebrating Christmas, which was two weeks away. Tennant lingered on our minds continually, as he did with all the Railers, I was sure.

He'd been released from the hospital, which was great news, but he hadn't gone home. The brain specialists had been adamant about him spending time in a traumatic brain injury rehab facility in Hershey. Tennant had not been happy about it, but between his mother who was staying with Tennant indefinitely so that Jared could go back to work, and his boyfriend, the surly young man was convinced to give the facility a chance. Two weeks. Just fourteen days and then, if his therapists and doctors agreed, he could go home and have therapy on an out-patient basis. There would be no hockey for Tennant Rowe for the remainder of the season, obviously. So now we were all praying that he'd recover enough to play next year.

Plans to visit Ten at the rehab center had been made for tomorrow. Bryan was still working through the tremendous guilt he felt, which was part of the reason I'd made plans for a dinner party. His billet parents and my parents. Coming here, to eat, for an early holiday meet and greet that had me as nervous as a tick on dip day.

"This tree is sad," Jess commented as I walked around my dingy table touching all the silverware to make sure they were straight. "Why do people even buy fake trees? Why not live ones? And why would you buy one someone with no design taste had decorated for you?" She plucked a glittery-gold gingerbread man off a bent limb and held it up by one arm. "This is truly hideous."

Garrett followed me around the table, pushing the silverware a tad to the left.

"Would you stop doing that?" I barked at my brother. He lifted an eyebrow. I blew out a long breath. "Sorry, sorry. The closer it gets to them walking through the door, the antsier I become."

"'Antsy' isn't the word that I'd use," my brother commented, then moved all the glasses a few inches to the right. The urge to swat the man in the neatly pressed three-piece suit was overwhelming. "More like neurotic."

I glanced at Jess. She nodded at her father's assessment of my behavior and then threw the glittery gingerbread man to Voodoo, named in homage to the Black Sabbath song of the same title, the black alley cat Bryan had invited in a few days ago. The cat had made himself at home and had taken to sleeping with us. We'd bathed him twice in flea shampoo the day he had moved in. Both of us had battle scars from that little endeavor. Voodoo swatted the decoration under the sofa, then walked off as if bored with the game, skinny black tail in the air.

"Okay, yes. I'm nervous. And when I get nervous, I get stressed. And when I get stressed, I get—"

"Neurotic," Garrett and Jess said at the same time.

I had a good comeback ready to fire when I heard feet coming up the stairs. Smacking Garrett's hand from the glass by my plate, I rushed to the door, my stomach filled with acid from my neurotic behavior no doubt. Bryan smiled at me when I flung the door open, inviting in snowflakes that were falling from the dark afternoon sky.

"We ran into your folks outside the shop. They were parked behind us," Bryan informed me, sneaking in a quick kiss, then stepping inside to allow the people with him to come in out of the cold.

There was this disconnect from me and the rest of the world for several long seconds when my mother and father hustled into my little place. Mom shook off the scarf she'd tied around her head, sending snow crystals flying to the floor. Then, her eyes touched mine.

In all the possible scenarios I'd ever imagined since we'd lost Gina, seeing my mother and father in this apartment had never dared to be envisioned. Yet here they were. Looking at me with tears in their eyes.

I vaguely heard Garrett clearing his throat. Mom bit down on her bottom lip, gaze full of sorrow. I went to her, hugged her, held her, and wept on her while she cried on me. Garrett and Jess stepped up. I released my mother so she could see her eldest son and hug the grandchild she had never met before. Dad shook my hand, his lips set and his eyes dewy. As Garrett had said, we'd never been demonstrative, and all the weeping and wailing my mother was doing now was probably enough to last my father for the next twenty years.

"We missed you boys," Dad said roughly, his grip tightening for a moment before he moved back to allow Bryan's billet parents to wiggle in for a warm greeting. Daisy and George were amazing people, outgoing and prone to smiling with ease. I could see why Bryan loved them as he did.

The meal was weird. Weird the way something feels surreal and yet you're living it, so you know it's happening because you can taste the meatloaf, smell the garlic potatoes, touch the heavy meat platter as you pass it to your niece, and see your family sitting across from you. Jess made up for the lack of conversation coming from Garrett and me. I did jump in from time to time, but the years spent apart, being hated, hung heavily over my head and would for some time to come. Garrett, well, he was Garrett. Dry as the Sahara but not rude. Bryan kept smiling awkwardly at me, his knee beside mine under the table. Overall, it was the first rough sketch of what, I hoped, would resemble a family again in the future.

After dessert, which was a red-and-white-marble cake Jess had baked, my parents left, citing an early morning flight out to Arizona to visit my mother's sister over the holidays. Bryan, Garrett and I got handshakes from my Dad and a peck on the cheek from my mother. Jess was hugged and had her cheeks pinched by her grandmother. Grandpa just gave her a quick hug and then led my mother back out into the cold.

Bryan's parents, I refused to think of them as "just his billet parents" because they were all the good things parents should be for him, stayed for coffee and chitchat until midnight when Bryan ran them to their hotel room. They were staying over for the game tomorrow night and would be flying back home at five in the morning the following day.

When it was just Voodoo and me, Garrett and Jess had stayed to help clean up, then left as well, I sat on the sofa, mentally spent but feeling a peaceful sort of sensation in my breast.

Motörhead's *Overkill* album was spinning on the turntable, Voodoo had draped himself over my sock-covered feet resting on the coffee table, and I had a cup of hot coffee and a stack of mail, mine and the mess that Bryan always grabbed at home and threw in with mine, to sort while I waited for Bryan to get back. Of course, I had no *fucking* idea where my reading glasses were, and I hated to disturb the cat purring away contentedly on my feet. Holding the top envelope out as far as my arm would stretch, I could just make out that it appeared to be a handwritten address with Bryan as the addressee. I saw that the return address had been written in a looping way that matched the mailing address.

Setting it aside, I then began opening my mail until my eyes burned from squinting. Bryan ambled in with snow covering his hair about ten minutes later. I might have dozed off but would never admit to doing so if asked.

"Sleeping?" he asked, shucking off his coat and kicking off his shoes to join me on the sofa.

"Nope."

"You're a bad liar," he said with a soft smile.

"Just checking my eyelids for holes."

"Right." He ran a hand over Voodoo, who purred loud enough to match Lemmy's vocals and then fell back into the cushion. I rubbed at my eyes and yawned. "Where are your DILF glasses?"

"No clue." I let my eyes close again because they were tired, and Bryan was warm and safely beside me. He shuffled around a bit. Then I heard the soft rip of paper, him tearing open an envelope. Sleep was creeping up on me when he made a sound like a wounded animal. I forced my weary eyes open and turned my head in his direction. His jaw was tight, his mouth in a frown. "Overcharged on your cable bill again?"

"It's a letter from my parents."

Sloppy and muddy with fatigue, I sat there wondering why his folks would have written to him when they'd been coming to see him. And who wrote letters anymore? Hell, the next generation wouldn't know how to write in cursive because of the invention of texting.

"Oh," I mumbled when the terse words sunk into my brain. "Your birth parents?"

It seemed odd to refer to them like that since Bryan had never really been given up or officially adopted by Daisy and George, but honestly, did legal stamps and court papers designate who we loved as family? Nope, they did not.

A hundred questions rested on my tongue, but I let him read in silence. Well, as silent as it could be with the Kilmister and his crew on the turntable.

"Shit," he finally said, the word an explosion of feeling on a shaky whisper. "They're not doing this to me, not again." He tore the letter in half, then in quarters, and then into smaller and smaller bits, until all that was left was a mound of confetti on the coffee table that Voodoo's thin tail stirred up as it lazily swept back and forth.

"Doing what?" I placed a hand to the back of his neck, the short hair on his nape as soft as a kitten's belly. I worked my fingers into the tense muscles.

"Anything. Just—"

"Hey, you don't have to tell me if you don't want to. I totally get how hard it is to rehash family stuff." God, did I ever.

"No, Mitch says in therapy that we need to talk about bad stuff." He lifted the cat from my feet, cuddled him under his chin, and then fell backward into the sofa, Voodoo limp as a wet rag in Bryan's big hands. "Talking about it gets it out and makes you deal with it all."

Ugh. Dealing with all my stuff would take years. I stared at my lover nuzzling an old alley cat and had to confess that he'd been doing a stellar job with his sessions. Maybe there was something to this whole 'talk it out with a professional' thing that I'd not seen or refused to recognize, before.

I ran my hand up into his hair. He liked that and responded as Voodoo would to a scratch on the chin. The stress lines around his mouth eased as I massaged his scalp.

"They kind of burn through cash," he said softly, his voice low. I turned on the sofa to face him, my fingertips working away the tension. "Since I turned pro, they've been hitting me up on occasion for money. I think they're spending it on scam preachers…maybe. I don't know. They say not, but yeah, it's been a thing for a year or two. I feel guilty for not helping them when they ask, but I know I shouldn't. They're using me, right?"

Well shit. "Yeah, maybe they are, babe." I cupped his head gently, easing him to me. I placed a kiss to the side of his head, inhaling the scent of his shampoo, wishing I had pretty words to comfort him better. "That shitty behavior of theirs is not on you though."

"Yeah, but I keep giving in because I think if I give them money, they'll love me as parents should."

He teetered to the side, him and Voodoo, and lay on my chest. I got them settled perfectly, his back to my chest and the cat lying across his throat like a black mink stole with a twitchy tail.

"You and I both know that we have no control over other people." I stroked his face, the back of my knuckles passing along his strong jaw.

"Yeah, I know."

His weight was enjoyable. I smiled at those long legs of his dangling over the arm of the couch.

"And we can't make our parents love us any more than we can make other people love us. It just hurts worse when it's our family that doesn't care because...well, they're family."

"Truth. I really don't need them to worry over my soul. My soul is in excellent hands. The same hands that hold my heart. *Your* hands."

"I just adore you."

He let himself melt into me. The record ended, and silence now filled our space. Even the cat had fallen still, his purrs drifting off as he slipped into a deep sleep. "You should think about talking to Mitch. He's good. He's really helping me."

"I know he is." Wow, that was curt. "I'm just not sure I'm ready to talk this all out with some stranger. I'm old and set in my ways and—"

"And making excuses."

Smartass kids. Jess had said the same thing to me not two days ago. Actually, she'd lambasted her father and me for bottling things up or suppressing things or whatever it was that we did that she felt was detrimental to our mental health.

"Yes, I'm making excuses." He tipped his head up and puckered his lips. I pressed my mouth to his for a moment. Voodoo reached up with an ebony paw to touch my chin.

I could imagine what the cat was thinking.

Ahem, hoomans, please do not make smooches upon each other when a perfectly good feline is willing to allow you to pay homage to his greatness with pets and kisses and a few crunchy cat treats.

Bryan chuckled softly at the cat. "I think we should get him a treat."

"I refuse to get up and get him treats," I said with as much false umbrage as I could muster. "I will pet his belly though."

"Cats aren't fond of belly rubs."

I slipped my hand under his shirt and moved my palm in a slow way over his firm stomach.

"You are though, yeah?" I asked, my voice getting all kinds of Sam Elliott gruff and sexy. Bryan nodded as his eyes drifted shut. A rather naughty vision of my hand slithering into his pants popped to life right before the cat leaped on that hand moving under Bryan's shirt.

Five minutes later as we were dumping peroxide on the back of my hand, I chanced a peek at Bryan fussing over the four deep holes in my skin.

"He's sorry," Bryan said, then placed a small, round Band-Aid to cat claw hole number one.

"He didn't look sorry."

"Maybe he needs another cat to play with?" Those sensual eyes of his lifted from his first aid work. I stared at him, knowing that this man could suggest we get an elephant for Voodoo to play with and I'd be out buying giant puppy piddle pads tomorrow. "You know, he's young, and he's got all this energy that he needs to get rid of."

"Hmm, not unlike someone else I know."

His gaze lit up with sexual promise. He then took an hour or so to show me just how much energy he really possessed. It was quite a lot.

.   .   .

THE NEXT DAY after the morning skate, we drove out to Hershey. Bryan had been adamant about seeing Tennant, and I was not about to deny him this…or much of anything.

The rehab facility was shiny and new, state of the art, and filled with smiling staff aiding those who had suffered terrible brain injuries down the sunny halls. Upon checking in at the visitor's desk, we were told that we could find Tennant in the western solarium and to follow the blue line on the floor.

We passed rooms that housed swimming pools, weights, and all manner of rehab equipment. The place was spotless, the floors buffed, the walls bright white with yellow wallpaper trim up by the ceiling.

Bryan hustled along, my hand in his, until the blue line on the sparkling floor ended outside a beautiful room filled with plants and walls of glass overlooking rolling lawns. At a table by a small rock fountain sat Tennant, his mother and Max van Hellren. I had a small fan moment upon seeing the retired star player seated across a checkerboard from Ten. I'd always loved the way Max had played hockey. We made our way across the room, stepping carefully around therapists and families visiting patients. Some of the patients were working with small balls, others were writing with pencils or chalk, with others trying to pick up little things that they then had to place into containers.

Tennant glanced up when we neared the round table. He smiled widely at us. Max craned his head to see what his checkers partner was smiling at. Then he rose and took Bryan's hand.

"Glad to see someone has decided to come out and take a turn. I'm tired of this pup whipping my ass." Max pumped Bryan's hand and then mine.

"He's full…uh…full of shit," Ten said, his voice nice

and strong, if still a little slurred. "I beat him…uh… maybe…uh…twice?"

"Right. Try like five times out of seven games." Max offered Bryan his seat, then lingered behind Mrs. Rowe, who was reading a book on an e-reader.

"Soon as Ben gets back from the manager's office, we're heading out. Nice to see the team keeping him in their thoughts," Max whispered to me as Bryan set up the board for another game, Tennant's faltering speech a sign that while the young man was better, he had a hell of a long way yet to go.

"He's never far from our thoughts, trust me."

Mrs. Rowe looked back at us and smiled sadly. Max patted her shoulder, then glanced up to see Ben walking toward us. I'd seen a few images of them together since Max's retirement. Talk about the dream life. Out on a farm with rescued farm animals and small pets.

"Sorry that took so long," Ben said after we'd been introduced. "We're hoping to set up a small animal visiting program or even have the patient's rehab feature caring for some rabbits that we've just rescued."

"That would be amazing," Bryan said as he waited for Ten to take a turn. It took the kid a bit of time, and you could see the frustration flaring up at his constant need to ask if he could move a certain way with no king. "Ben, you wouldn't happen to have any cats in need of a good home, would you? Ones that get along well with other cats?"

Max's handsome boyfriend smiled as if someone had handed him a winning lottery ticket.

"Bryan, let me tell you all about the cats we have that are looking for a good home."

Ben pulled a chair over to sit next to Bryan, who was the very picture of innocence. Max and I exchanged glances.

"Might as well have a seat, Gatlin. This may take a while," Max said with a knowing little wink.

I had nothing planned for the rest of the day and seeing that glow in Bryan's gaze made the next hour talking about cats and adoption papers fly past. Sort of. Okay, not really, but if it made Bryan happy, then I'd have sat there for a month.

Epilogue

Bryan

There was no two ways about it; the kittens had taken over our lives.

"Remind me again why we took two?" Gatlin muttered as he extricated kitty claws from his neck.

"Company," I reminded him and scooped Lemmy from Gatlin's outstretched hands.

He shook his head when the little fur ball wriggled free and launched itself at him again, this time using his Railers' jersey as a ladder, snagging the logo and up to his shoulder, where my number sat on the arm. Gatlin scooped him up and held him in one hand, the tiny kitten batting at his fingers. I caught the smile on his face; he could pretend he was annoyed by Lemmy and his sister, Fox, but I'd caught him sleeping on the sofa yesterday with both kittens curled on his chest and his hands reflexively and protectively holding them.

"C'mon little one," he murmured and carried him through to the small utility area that we'd made kitten-friendly. Fox had found an old hockey helmet, and that's where she slept, softly snoring and quite the opposite to Lemmy. Where Fox slept and ate and then slept again, Lemmy was a terror who wanted to get into everything.

He'd watched me in the shower from the mat, and I swear I saw intent in his eyes and made sure the glass door was firmly shut, aware that having a kitten climbing my naked body would not make the list of *good things*.

Finally, we could shut the door on them, and then it was time to leave for the arena. Tonight, we played Florida, and I was excited to be the starting goalie, with Jamie Rowe trying to get past me. I liked Ten's brother a lot, same as I did Brady, but hell, I was not going to let them get a goal on me. No way.

We were halfway down the stairs when I realized I'd forgotten my lucky coin. Every hockey player has a lucky something. Mine was a coin that Daisy had given me for the bus my first day with the billet family. My new *mom* wanted to make sure I had enough money, but I was too shy to get on the bus and had walked. We'd won a game that night, and ever since, the coin was always with me. Stupid I know, but there you go, we all cling to things that make us feel good.

"I'll start the car," Gatlin said and took off down the remaining stairs. He was coming with me to the arena, had a space in the family box, and had made fast friends with Connor's wife and kids. In fact, he was good with kids *and* kittens. A family man.

When I walked back into the apartment, my cell phone was ringing. I'd taken to leaving it there, noticing that the sound of it wrecked my concentration. Despite knowing that the telephone triggered memories of Aarni and the Raptors, I was still working through these issues.

I didn't mean to look at it, but a glance at the screen

and Aarni's name appearing there was enough to knock me sideways. I fought the need to instantly answer it in case I pissed him off, and it went to voicemail. My coin was where I left it, right next to my deodorant, and I pocketed it and began to leave.

Only the cell rang again.

I picked it up, and my thumb hovered over the "OK" to answer it. I didn't consciously recall my thumb connecting with the button, but it did, and I heard Aarni's voice.

"Finally you answer your damn phone," Aarni snapped. I placed the phone on the counter and stared at it. "Bryan? Bryan!"

Stepping back and away, I couldn't take my eyes off the damn thing.

"Bryan, are you there?"

I reached over and put the call on loudspeaker.

"I'm here," I finally said.

"Fuck's sake, Bryan, I've been trying to get hold of you."

I hadn't seen any missed calls, so this was only the second time he'd tried, and he was angry I hadn't answered straight away. An apology was on the tip of my tongue, but I forced it down. I was done apologizing and worrying where he was concerned.

"What do you want?" I asked instead.

"This is stupid. You saw what happened. I didn't deliberately hurt that asshole, but the fucking Railers won't let it go. I made a statement. What else does everyone want?"

I stayed quiet, and that was fuel on the fire.

"Fuck's sake, Bryan, tell your fucking asshole of a center to make a statement and get everyone off my back."

Ah. So that was what this was about.

I felt Gatlin beside me, and he curled his hand around

mine, lacing our fingers. He was everything to me, my strength, my love, my future, and I never knew I could ever love someone as deeply as I did Gatlin. I didn't rely on him for decisions or worry about what he thought. I wasn't scared of my own shadow when I was with him.

He made me stronger just by being in my life.

"Bryan, are you listening to me? Tell Ten to release a statement."

Gatlin squeezed my hand, and I glanced at him, seeing the compassion and concern in his eyes.

"No."

The word was so simple. I don't think I'd ever said *no* to someone before in quite the same way, not with such utter conviction.

"Bryan—"

"No, I won't tell Ten to do anything. You threatened him and me, and you deliberately dragged him over your skate and dropped him. You wanted to hurt him, not in the heat of battle but in a deliberate way."

"That's fucking bullshit—"

"You deserve everything you're getting. You're vindictive, threatening, controlling, and playing for a team that is rotten to the core, and I swear I am done with you."

I reached for the phone, cut him off mid-tirade, and ended the call.

Then I stood in silence for a few moments until Gatlin tugged me close and I went into his arms willingly, resting my cheek on his shoulder and inhaling the scent of him. I waited for the panic or the guilt, but instead, I felt lighter.

"I love you," I murmured, and tightened my grip on him.

He eased me away and then used the tip of his finger to tilt my chin.

"Love you more," he whispered. "Always."

Then hand in hand we left for the Arena, and goddamnit, I was going to stop every shot on goal. I could feel it in my bones.

I was invincible.

THE END

Next for the Railers

Neutral Zone (Harrisburg Railers #7, a novella)

Tennant Rowe has it all, a boyfriend he adores, a loving family, and a career on the rise. He's sure of his place in the world, and the future can only get brighter. Then one night, in a flash of skates and sticks, life changes forever. Getting back on the ice is Ten's priority, and experts tell him that it's just a matter of time.

Jared watches his lover fall in more ways than one, and when tragedy strikes, even the strongest of relationships are tested. Ten is strong, but Jared has to be stronger to help the man who holds his heart. Only, he has to admit that maybe it isn't just him who can make Ten whole again.

Jared and Ten's love is forever, but the rocky path to the romantic Christmas Jared had planned may be hard to travel.

Hockey Series' from RJ Scott & V.L. Locey

Harrisburg Railers

Owatonna U Hockey

Arizona Raptors

Boston Rebels

LA Storm

Chesterford Coyotes - Young Adult

Free Reads

Please note - in all of these free stories, there will be some spoilers for the main series books.

Railers Short Stories

Volume 1 | Volume 2

LA Storm

Sparkle

The Colts - AHL Short Stories

Pucks & Percentages

Breakaway

Making the Save

Standalone

Waiting for Christmas

Harrisburg Railers

When hockey wunderkind Tennant Rowe meets his new coach, he knows he's in trouble. Jared Madsen is nine years older than Tennant, impossibly attractive, and — worst of all — his brother's off-limits best friend. Is their chemistry worth the risk?

Changing Lines (Railers 1)

Can Tennant show Jared that age is just a number, and that love is all that matters?

The Rowe Brothers are famous hockey hotshots, but as the youngest of the trio, Tennant has always had to play against his brothers' reputations. To get out of their shadows, and against their advice, he accepts a trade to the Harrisburg Railers, where he runs into Jared Madsen. Mads is an old family friend and his brother's one-time teammate. Mads is Tennant's new coach. And Mads is the sexiest thing he's ever laid eyes on.

Jared Madsen's hockey career was cut short by a fault in his heart, but coaching keeps him close to the game. When Ten is traded to the team, his carefully organized world is thrown into chaos. Nine years his junior and his best friend's brother, he knows Ten is strictly off-limits, but as soon as he sees Ten's moves, on and off the ice, he knows that his heart could get him into trouble again.

Changing Lines

Harrisburg Railers (Hockey Romance)

1. Changing Lines
2. First Season
3. Deep Edge
4. Poke Check
5. Last Defense
6. Goal Line
7. Neutral Zone
8. Hat Trick
9. Save The Date
10. Baby Makes Three
11. Rivals
12. Perfect Gifts
13. Family First

Railers Volume 1 | Railers Volume 2 | Railers Volume 3 | Railers Volume 4

Meet the men of Owatonna University's hockey team

Ryker (Owatonna U, 1)

Ryker

Ryker is hockey royalty, Jacob is a poor country boy. Can two vastly different people find common ground and become the men they want to be?

Ryker comes from a long line of championship-winning hockey players. Playing college hockey to develop his game is his only focus, and nothing will stand in the way of him working to become the best player. He has no room for relationships, people who point out his flaws, or anyone who calls him on his dreams. He certainly has no place for love, and meeting Jacob is nothing but a useful distraction on the side. After all trying to get his Owatonna Eagles teammate into bed is less work and more play. When tragedy rocks his family, his charmed life crumbles, and the only person he can turn to is the same one who claims to hate him.

Jacob Benson has only known hard work and stifling conservative values his whole life. Born and raised in the small rural community of Eden Crossing, Minnesota, he's the only son of a hard-working but struggling dairy farming family. Jacob is using his skills in hockey to finance his way to an agricultural science degree. These four years at Owatonna U. will probably be the only time he has to enjoy life, gain acceptance about his sexuality, and live openly before his inevitable return to the farm. Running into a pretty rich boy like Ryker Madsen is putting a damper on his enjoyment of life away from home. Ryker's flip, conceited, carefree attitude grates on Jacob's every nerve. So why, if Ryker is everything he dislikes, does he want nothing more than to explore the sinful dreams that his annoying teammate stars in every night?

Ryker

Owatonna U Hockey (Hockey Romance)

1. Ryker
2. Scott
3. Benoit
4. Christmas Lights
5. Valentine's Hearts
6. Desert Dreams

Coast to Coast (Arizona Raptors 1)

Coast To Coast

When opposites attract, this bottom-of-the-league team will never be the same again.

A stipulation in his father's will forces Mark back into the arms of a family that disowned him and leaves him one-third owner of a hockey team facing financial ruin. He doesn't even watch hockey, let alone like it, and wants nothing more than to head back to New York. Then there's the new coach, a stubborn, opinionated, irritating man with superiority issues and questionable music taste. Butting heads with Rowen becomes the new normal, but it comes with passionate debate and an all-consuming lust.

Challenged to rebuild one of the worst teams in the league into a future cup contender, Rowen can't pass up the opportunity. Never in his twenty years of hockey has he ever seen a team managed so badly or coached players overflowing with resentment and bigotry. Yet there's something about this team and this city that compels him to roll up his sleeves and start dismantling. If only Mark, one of three siblings who now own the Raptors, wasn't so damned rock-headed yet so damned appealing his job might be easier. It doesn't look like either is willing to give in, but one night in a dark, desert hotel changes everything.

Coast To Coast

Arizona Raptors (Hockey Romance)

1. Coast To Coast
2. Across the Pond
3. Shadow and Light
4. Sugar and Ice
5. School and Rock

Boston Rebels

Top Shelf (Boston Rebels 1)

Acting on the attraction to his best friend's brother has always been off the table for Xander until a passionate hookup with Mason at a beach resort begins a love affair that burns long after summer ends.

Mason specializes in assisting same-sex couples on their journey to becoming parents and fighting every rule that blocks his way in the stuck-in-the-past agency that hired him. Living in his brother's pool house is rent-free, and every cent he earns he saves for his dream—that one day he'd have his own company helping others. The downside is that he has to see his annoying brother every day, the upside is that his brother's teammates from the Boston Rebels make regular visits. The eye candy that passes Mason's window is almost enough to make him consider dating a hockey player, but not just any player though. Ever since Xander —his brother's childhood friend—came out as gay at a press conference, Mason's puppy love has turned into a burning attraction he can no longer ignore.

Hockey has been one of Xander's main focuses since he was old enough to balance on skates. Well, hockey and Mason Kingsley, but Mason was always unattainable. Now that he's about to see thirty candles on his birthday cake and is no longer hiding the fact he's gay, he's ready to find a soul mate to make his life complete. A summer vacation is just what he needs to have time to think, but when the Boston Rebels arriving in paradise with Mason in tow, thinking is the last thing he needs. One torrid night under a balmy moon and rules about not messing with his best friend's brother vanish on a warm, tropical breeze.

Summer romances don't generally last past Labor Day, but with the new season about to begin Xander and Mason are going to have to face the world and decide if their love is real enough to withstand everything.

Boston Rebels

Lost In Boston (Free Prequel Novella)

1. Top Shelf
2. Back Check
3. Snowed
4. Royal Lines
5. Blade
6. Rental

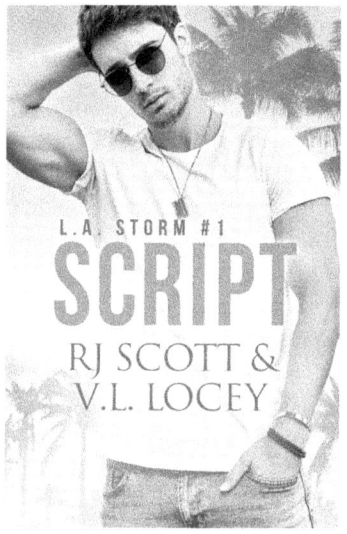

Script (LA Storm, 1)

Script

Hollywood A-lister Finn might be Canadian, but he needs Cameron to show him how to hockey.

Actor Finn Kerrigan is at a crossroads. After growing up a soap star, then starring in a hugely successful trilogy of action movies, he's finally given the chance to read a heartfelt and passionate script that could change his life forever. The role would be enough for people to see him as a serious actor, and maybe even win him an award or two (and no, a golden raspberry award for his action movies doesn't count). Once established as a serious actor he's sure he can come out of the closet and finally live his truth. When he lies to get the part of a hockey player on a struggling team, he suddenly has nowhere to hide. He might be Canadian, but the last time he skated he was ten, and no, he doesn't have hockey in his blood. With only a month until filming starts, he about to be exposed, but partnered with a player who's supposed to be giving him tips, he doesn't realize how many of his secrets will come to light. Falling in lust, one heated kiss at a time, is inevitable, but giving Cameron up at the end of the shoot could break his heart.

Cameron Chavkin is the face of the LA Storm. And the body, and the hair, and the smile. He's at the prime of his career, men and women want to be with him, and he's skating better than he ever has before. His house sits next to a famous rock star's mansion, his garage is filled with expensive cars, and he's even been asked to mentor a once-famous actor in a new hockey movie. Life is pretty sweet. Until the bad boy of hockey meets Finn, a man on the edge with more secrets than Cameron has endorsements. Knowing better than to get involved, Cameron is swept up despite himself, and when it's time to say goodbye to the Storm's most eligible bachelor is finding it hard to follow the script.

Script

LA Storm

1. Script
2. Second
3. Shield
4. Spiral

Off The Ice (Chesterford Coyotes, 1)

Off The Ice

A coming-of-age love story with high school, hockey rivalry, friendship, family, and coming out.

Soren's life changes in an instant when he and his younger brother are adopted by hockey royalty. Making sense of his new life is hard enough, but when he's enrolled in a private school it means facing a whole new set of problems. Navigating friendship, family, and hockey is one thing, but being attracted to the boy who vexes him is a whole new thing.

Felix has a reputation to protect. He's the kid who seems to have everything but looks can be deceiving. Spinning lies about his perfect life, he's created a fantasy world that even he has started to believe. Only, it's not long before everything crumbles, all of his pretty lies are revealed, and only his closest rival sees through his pain and stands by him.

Fighting is easy, friendship is hard, but love is everything.

Off The Ice

Chesterford Coyotes

1. Off The Ice
2. On Thin Ice
3. *Dance on Ice*

Also By RJ Scott

For a full list of ebooks and links please scan the code above or
visit rjscott.co.uk/rjbooks

Meet RJ Scott

RJ discovered romance in books at a very young age and realized that if there wasn't romance on the page, she could create it in her head. With over one hundred and fifty books published, she is a full time author of gay romance.

She lives and works out of her home in the beautiful English countryside, spends her spare time reading, watching films, and enjoying time with her family.

The last time she had a week's break from writing she didn't like it one little bit and has yet to meet a box of chocolates she couldn't defeat.

www.rjscott.co.uk | rj@rjscott.co.uk

NEWSLETTER - rjscott.co.uk/rjnews

facebook.com/author.rjscott

x.com/Rjscott_author

instagram.com/rjscott_author

amazon.com/author/rj-scott

bookbub.com/authors/rj-scott

goodreads.com/rjscott

pinterest.com/rjscottauthor

Also By VL Locey

For a full list of ebooks and links please scan the code above or visit vllocey.com/stories-from-vl-locey

Meet V.L. Locey

V.L. Locey loves worn jeans, yoga, belly laughs, walking, reading and writing lusty tales, Greek mythology, the New York Rangers, comic books, and coffee.

(Not necessarily in that order.)

She shares her life with her husband, her daughter, one dog, two cats, a flock of assorted domestic fowl, and two Jersey steers.

When not writing spicy romances, she enjoys spending her day with her menagerie in the rolling hills of Pennsylvania with a cup of fresh java in hand.

vllocey.com
vicki@vllocey.com

Newsletter - vllocey.com/newsletter

facebook.com/V.L.Locey

x.com/vllocey

instagram.com/vl_locey

bookbub.com/authors/v-l-locey

goodreads.com/vllocey

pinterest.com/vllocey